Copyright © 2024
All rights reserved. No part of this publication may be reproduced, distributed, or transmitted in any form of by any means, including photocopying, recording, or other electronic or mechanical methods, without the prior written permission of the author, except in the case of brief quotations embodied in critical reviews and certain other noncommercial uses permitted by the copyright law. For permission requests, write to the author, addressed "Attention: Permissions Coordinator," at the address below.

ISBN: 979-8-218-65328-6

Library of Congress Control Number: TBD

Front Cover image by Andrew Bennett

Book design by Andrew Bennett

Printed by KDP, in the United States of America

First printing edition 2025

Andrew Bennett
Axis Admirals Hill
Chelsea, MA 02150

This is a work of fiction.

Names, characters, places, and incidents are either the product of the author's imagination or used fictitiously, and any resemblance to actual persons, living or dead, businesses, companies, events, or locales is entirely coincidental.

To My Bad Bunch
Who always kept it crazy

And to My Wife
Who always kept it sane

Track 1: Intro

Funerals don't feel like funerals without rain. If movies have taught us anything, and I'd like to think they've taught us a great deal, is that when someone proper and important shuffles off this mortal coil the weather will act accordingly. Gray and thick with fat raindrops that wash off all the black umbrellas and soak into the black suits underneath. A graveyard sky. Funeral weather. Bleak and midnight dreary. If a person is class enough, and is to be mourned enough, the sky is required to pay homage.

Weeping as those below weep.

It's pretty tough tits that at this funeral it's a sweltering eighty-nine and sunny. I don't know if the film industry has lied to us or if the person in the hole just wasn't up to the whole sky mourning dramatically snuff.

Say what you will about Brandon Lake, but he was class enough to me.

So, the weather can go suck it.

But then again if you think about it, and I mean really think about it, maybe the movies had it right all along. Maybe there would be rain if this had been a well and true funeral. Yes, there is a hole. And yes, there is a coffin and tombstone and sure there are black suits. But if funerals don't feel like funerals without rain, then they sure don't feel like funerals without a stiff either.

The weather probably would have cooperated a bit more had there been an actual body in the box.

Missing and presumed dead.

AR Bennett

Dead enough for this dog and pony show. Dead enough for the time being. Dead as dead can be. My friend was never one for convention. Never toed the line or walked the right path. Of all people he'd be the one to be late to his own funeral. Or not even bother to show up at all. That all tracked.

So,

Brandon Lake was dead to begin with.

That was very Dickens of me. Not what you'd expect from yours truly, of that, I'm sure. What can I say? Funerals bring out the literary in me. But it's true. Or, true enough for the time being. Brando was gone. Of course, the Brandon I knew had been gone for a while. They say it takes a long time for stars to burn out. Hell, we wouldn't even know until something like eight or nine minutes passed if all of a sudden, our sun just up and winked out. Eight minutes to even notice the flaming nuclear reactor in the sky was now nothing more than a darker than dark spot set in the blackness of the void. The bigger the star, the longer it takes to fade into oblivion.

And like I said, Brandon Lake was class. The closest thing this decrepit town had to a true star.

Now he was gone. Truly gone. Gone enough for a gravedigger to cash a paycheck. That darkness took a bit to hit me. To sink in. Which is why I'm standing here staring down at a patch of dry dirt sweating through a monkey suit in the blistering heat long after all the other mourners in black have slunk off to find the shade and a/c. Just me and an empty box and a fresh dug hole.

I'm not one to live in the past. I'm a bit more of this very moment type guy. Carpe Diem. And sometimes - okay a great many times if I'm being honest - Carpe Noctem. Seize the day. Or the night. Whatever time needed seizing. I know that right now is all I'm ever going to get. But you're not here for philosophy. No no no. Plots by their very nature have to move forward. And we will. Jesus. Can't a guy get a few moments to mourn his friend?

There will be plenty of time to run all night of that I promise you. It's coming. Okay? But for right now let me just…

…process.

Yes, Brandon is gone. I've come to terms with that. I've even come to terms with how he got here. In this hole. Sure, the gravedigger did the work but Brandon was really the one who dug this for himself. We all knew it. And none of us needed hindsight being 20/20 to see it coming. This train was off the tracks for a long time. Time to move on. And yeah, okay. I can do that and I've probably moved on more than some of the other people who stood around this dusty plot of faded yellow grass. But it's not what *wa*s that needs processing. It's what's *next*.

There's the wake.

Obviously.

Beyond that though, it's a bit of a grab bag. We've made it this far partly because Brandon Lake has always acted as a sort of guardian devil for our little enterprise. Even when he was off doing God knows what or where his contributions to a group he helped found was never far. He'd been there. Except now he wasn't.

Let's not get too dramatic about it here. Things were in the works. I had seen this coming after all. Saw the writing on the wall. Read the headline before the ink dried. Coming up with a plan is one thing. Dealing with the certainty of having to put said plan in action is another.

If we couldn't rely on Brandon Lake's certified platinum parachute we'd have to find our own way. And I'm no stranger to finding my own way.

AR Bennett

The beer in my hand tasted like tomorrow was going to be a rough one. Hell of a trip. It was going to get weirder. The Italians and the Armenians and the various groups from down South all under one roof. Then there's the groupies and the diehard fans. The columnists. The lawyers. The

Just

All of it.

Luckily anyone in the know and from our side of the tracks knows that a wake is an unofficial cease fire. Pay respects and let bygones be by and gone. For a night anyways.

After that…well after that it's anyone's guess. The wolves are certainly at the door.

The cigarette at my lips tastes like rituals unfulfilled. I breathe the smoke until only an ashy cherry is left, stick out my tongue, and with a deep sadness extinguish the butt against it. Barely grimacing as the ember sizzles on my mouth muscle.

For you man.

"Let's go get drunk." I raise the longneck to toast an empty graveyard. The beer helps ease down the ash and wet paper that I'm chewing into fine pulp. Helps with the burning sensation on my tongue. I tilt it back and chug down the remainder. Then I chuck the glass bottle at Brando's tombstone hard enough for it to shatter into thousands of jagged pieces glinting against the sun's glare scattered throughout the grass.

I stuff my hands in my pockets and start making my way to the only place I've ever called home.

'Bout that time.

Let's get this party started right and proper.

Track Two: The Shape of Punk To Come

Dawn at the Kelso Beach House comes in two forms.

The first is the gradual departure from the night where things are almost forced by the very nature of the sun rising to start settling down. The music is still going but the songs are slower. A collection of diehards and late nighters grudgingly admit they've burned the candle at both ends down to the wick and stumble out into the bright lights of a new dawn coming over the water.

The other dawn?

Well, that's basically hell.

Sunlight ripping through hastily closed blinds. Echoing of birds chirping blasting off like the rattattat of gunfire on some French hill crammed to the baguettes with zee Germans. This isn't sunrise. It's a nuclear explosion. Air heavy with stale smoke that chokes the tongue. Eyeballs caked in gunk and goo. Simultaneously hellishly hot and frigidly cold.

These are the hungover mornings. The gone-too-hard the night before mornings. The I-wish-I'd-just-stayed-dead mornings.

This dawn?

This is one of those mornings.

I'm no stranger to a life well wasted, but even I have my limits. A wake, especially an Irish wake, being one of them. Every groan of the old beach house hits like a hammer to the temple. Every lingering scent of scotch, smoke, and sin is a burning affront to my nose. I'm wondering if I really did overdo it and woke up paralyzed from the waist down, but then I'm wondering how the hell did my pants get on backwards with one leg wedged along with the other in one leg of pants. Pant?

Point is I feel a lot like how Jack Nicholson looks right now.

Not Chinatown Jack either. Twelve beers too many at a Lakers game Jack. Incidentally this thought brings up a hasty solution to the atomic inferno streaming from the open window. Look like Jack looks. Time to don the sunnies.

Only problem is my shades aren't where they should be. Instead, my fingers flop around on the nightstand until I scorch off a few fingerprints on a still smoldering cigarette crushed out in a cereal bowl.

It takes an effort that is either Sisyphean or Herculean to drag my corpse out of bed and my brain is too scrambled to figure out which Greek myth is the metaphor I'm looking for here.

Either way I'm not upright for long.

In the twenty seconds of time spanning the entirety of the lifecycle of the universe from big bang birth to the inevitable heat death it took me to get up and out I've bed I've already forgotten the predicament with my pants. There's a sudden nausea-inducing inner ear failure, a topsy turvy spinning sensation that starts at my toes, and then the floor tastes like sand, worn pine, and regret.

It's amazing how often regret tastes like bad pennies.

I just let the cool floor press against my face and the blood from the bit lip drool out in a puddle.

This feels nice.

This is my home now. I live here now. One with the floor and the sand and the copper twang of blood. Would you believe I've been in this exact situation at least six times before? Well maybe not *exact*. The pants thing is relatively new.

I'm not a big fan of suits.

Probably for this exact reason.

Or maybe, the floor seems to ask, having decided to be extra chatty this morning, you're not a fan of suits because out of the two you own, the black one gets used the most. Not a lot of people are getting married in your circle these days.

"Shut the hell up, floor." I mumble through gritted teeth spitting out a chunk of my inner lip.

The floor doesn't say anything else. It's a floor. What the hell else has it got to say?

Though it doesn't offer any more sage wisdom it does lose its alluring coolness and starts smelling like sick and sweat and all the other charming aromas of a debilitating hangover. Takes me a bit longer than it should to realize it's not the floor's fault.

It's me.

I manage to get my pants off by caterpillaring my way around until they just sort of slide off. Then there's the boot camp style crawl to the bathroom. The tumble into the shower. The heaving, panting, struggle of turning on the faucet and the molar cracking blast of ice-cold water hitting my face and physically assaulting my soul.

I'll save you the bits where I halfheartedly attempt to grind Irish Spring into my nuts and under my pits or the parts where I struggle to towel off using a frayed beach towel. Hell, I'll even skip the part where I stand dripping wet and staring into the mirror at a brand spanking new shiner under my left eye.

We'll just fast forward through that.

By the time I pull on a pair of boardshorts and a black band tee, the birds have stopped chirping. Which implies this all took even longer than I thought and its now suddenly late afternoon, or the construction crews are just about to clock in.

Then the jackhammers start and my head explodes as if I'm a news anchor in *'Scanners'*.

Eight AM. On the nose.

Like clockwork.

The rickety wooden stairs leading down from the collection of bedrooms presents a new challenge. I have to blink a few hard times to get them to stop spiraling into infinity and kaleidoscoping around. The only thing keeping me on task is the divine scent of coffee wafting up from down below.

If it wasn't for that it would be happy horror funhouse time all the way back to bed.

"Saint," Scooby nods as I stumble into the kitchen. "You look like hell."

There are two types of people in the world. Those that get nicknames and those that give them. Personally, I'm the latter and when coming up with my name I wanted to choose something to live by and up to. I chose Saint.

Not because I'm saintly.

God no.

But because I'm holey.

As in: "look at him. He's full of holes."

If you're not quite getting what I'm putting down let me paint a better picture. See there was this kid, ballsy reckless little shit, who always had a knack for trouble. Had a knack for extreme sports too. Things that go fast and fall hard. Has watched enough movies to think he'd make a good enough action hero too. Falls. Scrapes. Cuts and bruises. A baker's dozen broken bones. Little bro wears the scars like badges of honor. Gets good at mastering the pain. Takes a few dares and cashes a few bets, and next thing you know there's a string of cigarette burns down his arm. A string of nearly perfect circular

Holes.

See what I mean? Holy.

Nicknames aren't exactly rocket surgery. Take a person's prominent feature or dominant trait and craft something witty around it. The good ones are the ones that stick. Know enough people, build a big enough circle, and coming up with clever names is second nature. Besides, who amongst us doesn't want to be someone else on occasion.

"We're all heading that way eventually, Scoob." I groan as I ease myself into a bar chair. "Might as well look the part."

It's amazing how often a good nickname comes to be because of how you look. We all know a chunky fella named "Slim", or a short dude that goes by "Titan" or some such nonsense. Hell, there once was a guy with no arms and no legs floating in the lake. Went by Bob. Without a good nickname what's separating us from the animals? What kind of world would it be if we all went around as Larry, Ted and Terry?

Take Scooby for example.

Odd name for a guy who's not a dog. Never was a dog. Will never be a dog. Doesn't even look like a dog. But looks close enough to someone who'd own a dog – specifically a great big goofy Great Dane – that I, and by that extension everyone else, calls him Scooby.

He's tall and lanky with skinny parts where I'd have a bit of bulk. Dark haired and scruffy. Some call it brooding. Shadowy. Your classic opposite to our Hollywood B movie hero type. If I flourish in the spotlight, Scooby basks in the shade.

We've got a touch of the Odd Couple about us in that way.

Funny how that works out isn't it?

He just nods and slides a chipped mug across an equally chipped counter. I wrap my hands around it like the poor orphan Oliver and watch in nearly pornographic fixation as he pours black steaming life into the cup.

"You want eggs?"

Oh yea. Eggs. That's that smell.

I lift up a finger to have him hold that thought before rushing off the stool and out the back door. I make it down the sandy driveway before all the bile building at the back of my throat comes crashing out my mouth and nose.

There's something about someone projectile vomiting in a way that would make Linda Blair jealous that makes a person stop and stare. Even if those people are hardened, burly, construction dudes.

The jackhammering thankfully fades. Even if for a brief moment.

I wipe snot and puke off my face with the back of my hand before offering a devil-may-care smile and jaunty stringy slime coated wave at the foreman who just so happened to be getting out of his shiny new pickup.

He clutched that venti double shot mocha latte as if it was a child and there were only two spots left off the titanic.

"Morning Jimmy."

Jimmy, who has repeatedly told me his name is Bill, stares at me as if a squid just crawled out of my mouth. Which quite possibly it had.

"Don't worry! The boys from the city checked and the radiation isn't as bad as they thought." I blow a fat snot bubble and gag out another few heaves of last night's rager in a vaguely leather loafer direction. Jimmy takes a step back horrified. "Symptoms should go down soon! Take care Jimmy!"

I walk back into my beach house with a chuckle despite my insides now being on my outsides.

Scooby is frying bacon in a pan to go along with the eggs. He isn't exactly smirking because Scooby doesn't smirk, but he's not not either. Ever since these jabronis in hard hats showed up next door I've made it my personal mission in life to make theirs a living hell. Scoob knows this. And maybe even on some level he respects it. Embraces it a bit. Even if it is just in his Scooby sort of way.

"Get any on his shoes?"

"I tried man." I sigh disappointed before sliding back into a bar stool and picking up my coffee. "Gotta work on the arc. Really comes from the back of the throat."

There's that bitter taste of black coffee scolding my tongue. Hot bean water pummels my tonsils until it percolates down my gullet into my internal organs. Somewhere along the way the caffeine binds to my…you know what I'm not a doctor. It's hot, strong, and has enough go juice to make the fog in my head part slightly.

"We doing a keg and eggs or something? Why are you suddenly Susie Homemaker?"

"I figured the guys could use some breakfast. After," Scooby stops and sees my expression is dangerously close to don't finish that thought. "After you know."

AR Bennett

Burying an empty box where my dead friend should be? Dealing with all that mess? Yeah, I know.

"Where is everyone then?"

"Alaska and Benny Bones are doing calisthenics on the beach." He points with a spatula in a loosely thataway direction before returning to cooking.

As he cooks, he cleans any splats and spots he makes. I meanwhile purposely set my coffee cup off the coaster and directly onto the counter. Like I said, Odd Couple.

"HB?"

"Don't know." Scooby shrugs skinny shoulders without turning around. "Saw him with some groupies last night. You know him."

"Yeah yeah."

We talk a bit more about the other members of our little group while I switch the coffee around to get the taste of sick out of my mouth. This is the idle morning chit chat of two longtime friends, one of whom is insanely hungover. It isn't until the last drop of black gold has burned its way down my throat that I get serious.

"We gotta talk about that thing."

"What thing?"

"The thing Scoob. You know exactly the thing." I motion for him to reload the mug. "I'm going to need at least four more of these before you can start acting coy. The Plan. We discussed it last night."

Both the T and the P are capitalized even as the words come out of my mouth. The Plan. The words seem to hang in the air and float toward the lofty heights of the wood beams holding up a sagging ceiling. Scooby seems to study them as they float.

He pours another cup from the pot and shrugs. Out of habit he strokes his dark beard with his free hand. It's something he does when he's thinking, and he does it especially when he is thinking I'm about to do something stupid. His dark eyes meet mine even if my baby blues are struggling to see him clearly past a hangover that won't quit and sunlight that won't stop streaming through the windows.

"It's risky."

"It's really not." I sigh from my head on the counter.

"You know it even exists?"

"Oh, don't mother hen me with your hands on your hips like that Scoob."

I don't need to look up to see he's shaking his head and bringing his hands up off his hips to cross them across his thin chest. If it wasn't for the unholy cacophony of construction noises coming from the window the sound of his shoe tapping on linoleum would be deafening.

"To quote *'Maximum Rock N Roll'*: The long awaited third album is expected to be a tour de force set to light the punk world ablaze. Plus, you know as well as I do, he wrote the damn thing upstairs."

"Who's the buyer?"

"I got that. Just know there is one."

"Anyone I know?"

This isn't from Scooby. Unless he got real feminine real quick. I lift my head up from the counter to see Watson standing seductively in the doorway. She's got shopping bags in one hand and a cardboard coffee cup in the other.

"Where'd you go?"

"Shopping." She nods down to the bags in her hand. Which checks out. "I went to the mall and grabbed some new swimsuits."

"It is eight in the morning." I snort. "Is the mall even open?"

"It is for me." She states and you know what? I believe her. Watson's got that thing about her. "So, what's this job?"

Scooby sets the bacon on a neatly folded napkin on top of a plate. He lines up each piece precisely before wiping any residual grease off the counter. I can practically feel a faint electric current coming off him when he sees the brown coffee ring on the counter where my cup was. He watches Watson just as carefully.

Scoob's always careful, I just wonder what's up with whatever this is between these two. Now, however, is not the time. This is hangover time and right now I need a swim and maybe, probably, definitely a beer.

"Right. Here's the plan. Watson and I are going for a swim."

"Now?" She's asking but the smile on her face tells me she already said yes.

"No time like the present. Scoob," I say, turning to my right-hand man. "Get the Bunch back here. We've got work to do."

*****

Saint. Scooby. Watson. Maybe you're sensing a pattern here. Nicknames are important. They let people know you belong to somewhere where that moniker makes sense. Sometimes someone picked it for you, or maybe you're like me and you came up with it all on your lonesome.

Sometimes though the name that sticks isn't the one that you can take credit for. Or even want. Sometimes it's something you are branded with and just have to go on living up to. Such is the case with The Bad Bunch.

As in: "Stay away from them, they're a bad bunch."

I don't get credit for that one. No, that one came from truancy officers, teachers, cops, judges, and pretty much everyone else on the right side of the law and the good side of the tracks. Beats the *Little Rascals,* I guess.

What did Jessica Rabbit say? "I'm not bad. I'm just drawn this way."

In the grand calculus of society, we're not all bad. Yes, ninety percent of what we do on a daily basis would probably be considered unethical at best and flat out illegal at worst, but bad is a scale. There's smuggling pre-teens into the country via shipping containers bad, and then there's our brand of bad. Which is decidedly not that.

Do we break a few laws? Yes. Do we raise a bit of hell? Undoubtedly. But if there is black and white The Bad Bunch operates in the gray.

Some people work in the oil business. Some people work in pharmaceuticals. Others still might work in finance. That doesn't mean those people are clubbing baby seals, selling opioids to kids, or foreclosing on homes on Christmas Eve. The world's more complicated than that.

There's right and wrong and then there is everything else you gotta do to get by.

Among the many things I've done to get by, the most profitable is being in the connection business. It pays to know a guy who knows a guy. Sometimes that guy knows of something that might just fall off a truck if you get my gist.

And sometimes that guy who knows a guy who knows a guy might just point you in the direction of a guy who knows of a dilapidated beach house that's not on the market but could definitely use a new owner along with a new coat of paint.

AR Bennett

If you're going to sell things that fall off of trucks, having a place to sell those things out of is key. Someplace away from prying eyes and listening ears. Someplace that can well and truly be yours.

If you can host parties all night without the cops being called and have Lake Erie as your backyard to swim off the ensuing hangover in, then all the better.

Even the Little Rascals needed a clubhouse.

And it's a hell of a clubhouse too.

Two story beachy cape cod with a wide wrap around porch that faces the water. Is she the prettiest girl on the beach? Not really. Especially considering all the cookie cutter condo McMansions popping up down the way. But this old gal's got charm.

The paint was once sky blue before a summer storm when it was first painted but has since been bleached driftwood white by years of summer suns and winter freezes. All of the storm shutters are either stuck open or stuck shut, and there is no rhyme or reason to which is which. The wrap around porch is uneven. There's a plank missing here or there too. You can tell the contractors who built the place way back when were probably drunk because every angle that should be a flat ninety is off by just a degree or two.

To me she's beautiful.

Call it rose tinted glasses. Call it romanticism. To me there's no better place in the world. We go together like jigsaw pieces. The vibe here matches my vibe. Both of us are a bit too Hollywood for a small town but a bit too small town for Hollywood. We've got our scars. But we've got style. Call it whatever you want, but I'd call it love.

That's because the Kelso Beach House is home. And there's no place like home.

Which is why I'm trying to save it.

"It's never that easy Saint and you know it." Scooby states firmly. He's been pacing a hole in the faded wood floor since hearing my brilliant plan.

I've finished my swim and given enough time for the other members of the Bunch to trickle in. It's not all of us, mostly just the key players plus a few bar flies who know we're the only spot in town selling vaguely cold beer this early in the morning on a day that isn't St Patrick's Day. We've amassed a hell of a collection of misfits over the years. People on the wrong side of the tracks. People with nowhere else to go. Dirty. Tattooed. Uncivilized.

Our kind of people.

"I'm not seeing how it's that hard either my guy."

While Scooby paces back and forth, Watson and I are at a card table that's still covered in the debris of last night's festivities. Wake. Whatever. Empty Corona bottles and scattered playing cards. She's in my lap despite there being plenty of open seating options. Her fingers run through my damp hair in a way that is making it hard to concentrate on Scooby's objections.

"What about the guards?"

"What about them?"

"Well, the fact they exist for one thing." Scooby sighs and throws up his hands. He runs his own fingers through his own long dark hair and shakes his head. There's a nervous energy about him.

Which makes sense. Scoob isn't what you'd call a center of attention type of guy. He prefers the shadows which suit his personality and appearance just fine. He's the ying to my yang.

AR Bennett

I'm the center of the limelight sandy blonde sort of guy and he is the backstage brunette keeping the show running. I eat up screen time by chewing through dialogue while he says exactly what he needs to and not much more. I'm left, he's right. I'm south, he's north.

It's why we work so well together.

We're partners after all. Not in the holding hands having picnics sense, not that there's anything wrong with that, it's just not our vibe. One usually follows the other is all.

"Was there a follow up to that or what?"

"What?"

"Well, you said "for one thing". I just sort of assumed there'd be a second thing…ya know what? that's not important. Alaska can handle the guards. Isn't that right Alaska?"

While Scooby has been pacing and I've been sitting getting my scalp massaged by French pressed nails, Alaska and Benny Bones have taken up a game of beer pong to pass the time. At the mention of his name the big man turns his attention from the game, this in turn gives Benny Bones an opportunity to sneak in a cheeky bounce shot worth two cups.

Bones flashes a confident smile and gives me the double finger guns wink of a man happy to have a well-timed assist. I fire a finger gun back at him, happy to be of assistance. Alaska groans and picks up each cup in his large hands and proceeds to chug the first.

"What do I gotta do?" He burps before starting in on the second cup of beer.

"There's three of them." Scooby interjects before I can answer. He gives Alaska and Bones a look that asks if they should really be drinking at ten in the morning on a Tuesday.

I'm not one to talk. I'm already on my second Corona. Except mine is medicinal. Take two hairs of the dog that bit you and call me in the morning type deal.

"How rough?" Alaska asks after finishing his second cup and slamming it on the table.

"Just a black eye. Nothing serious."

Alaska looks between me and Scooby and shrugs his broad shoulders. "Not a problem."

"See Scoob. Not a problem."

We call Alaska 'Alaska' because he is the biggest state in the union. He's a full head and shoulders taller than everyone else in the bunch and just as broad.

Remember what I said about nicknames?

Similarly, Benny Bones is Bones because there was a time when he was just skin and. Even though now he's on a regiment of daily exercises and protein shakes the name sort of just stuck.

"They have guns."

"Who has guns?"

Scooby's face has gone a shade of red that isn't exactly crimson but it's close enough that it is on the same section at Home Depot. He clenches his bony knuckles together a few times before fixing me with a please for the love of God be serious stare. "The guards."

"Little ones or like AKs?"

"Does it matter?"

"I'd imagine it matters a great deal to Alaska. Isn't that right Alaska?"

"I'm not falling for that one again Saint." The big man calls over his shoulder. The game is progressing and Bones's side has decidedly more cups. "Bones if you can't beat me without your brother's help then I suggest you have him play me instead of you."

"All's fair, big man." Bones laughs and sinks another shot.

"I've got next then." I say to Alaska even though I'm fairly certain if I called on the winner I'd be playing against Bones. "You want in on this?"

Watson laughs and pulls on my ear with her fingers. "Loser goes skinny dipping?"

"Pretty sure that'd be Alaska."

"Fine by me."

"What?" Alaska and I echo simultaneously. The Big Man has taken his attention off the game and that's all young Bones needs to sink another shot. Watson laughs and it's her turn to fire a few finger guns Bones's way for the assist. She blows Alaska a kiss before turning back to me with a smirk.

Not sure I love that.

"Can we please get serious here?" Scooby snaps. He sits down at the card table with a huff and folds his arms against his chest. "What you're planning isn't a plan. It is B&E with some GSWs thrown in."

B&E. As in: 10-62. Entering unlawfully with criminal intent. Breaking and Entering.

GSWs. As in: A penetrating injury sustained from a projectile. Or in even plainer English: Gun Shot Wounds.

I grind my back teeth together and force the lingering headache to migrate to anywhere other than the thinking portion of my brain. A solid part of the interactions between the two of us are based around me saying a plan, proposal, course of action, whatever is doable while Scooby stands firm and fast stating no that plan, proposal, course of action, or various whatevers are in fact not doable.

I've found over the course of our very long friendship and partnership in crime that sometimes the best way to get things to go my way is to add a bit of cinema je ne sais quoi. Let's be honest here, we're the generation raised under the warm silver glow of movies, cable tv shows, and late-night music videos. Has this steady diet of pop culture somehow altered our brain chemistries and overwrote basic core functions of a thinking-based individual? Yeah. Probably. But even the best highbrow experts will yell from the mountain tops the fundamental rule of storytelling:

Show. Don't. Tell.

I pat Watson on the butt signaling that she needs to scoot. It's my turn on center stage. She gives me a bemused look before standing and fixing the parts of her bikini that have pinched in places I gotta admit I'm rather fond of. Stretching I crack my neck and knuckles until they pop with satisfying clicks and clacks before walking to the center of the open living room turned bar.

As if on cue the ancient jukebox comes to life with a crackle of faulty wiring and the barely recessed speakers snap to life after a hiss of static. A building punk beat fills the air, slowly and softly at first, but increasing in tempo with each step I step toward my rightful spot at center stage.

"What do you think, Bones? Scoob just needs to see the vision?" I ask as the flickering overhead lights click off one by one until only the one I am standing directly under remains. Bones smiles a toothy grin and shakes his head causing a cluster of blond curls to shake about loosely.

"Hell yeah brotherman."

I nod and give him a thumbs up. "Alaska?"

"Scoob could use a bit of the ol 'Oh Captain my captain'."

Now I've got my attention back on Scooby. He's massaging his temples in slow rhythmic circles and clockwise precise patterns.

"He's got no cajónes boys. Our Scooby. No vision. He wants to know 'The Plan'? Let's give it to him. Both barrels."

"Please don't."

"Oh, come man! Even Watson is feeling this." I turn to her and wink. "You're game for some grade A cinema yeah?"

She nods. "I'm always down to make a movie, Saint."

"Maybe later." I chuckle with a wink. That one is definitely going in my back pocket. "You just need to see the vision, Scoob."

"We're not doing this." He groans before banging his head thrice on the table.

"Too late for that amigo." I grin that trademark grin and send an arrogant buckle up buttercup wink Scooby's way. Black bars begin to press in from the top and bottom forcing the grainy gritty clarity of the real world into a compressed magazine gloss. Mega cool cinema style. The Golden Age of Hollywood at its finest. The oh too real of the unreal presses in. "This is happening."

The tempo from the speakers picks up steadily. Anticipation grows.

"Ready Scoob?"

"No."

Well, it's too late for that now isn't it. Things are already in motion. The ball is already rolling. Whether Scooby likes it or not this is happening. He just needs to see the vision. See what I see and how I see it. Then he will get it. That's how this works. Is it fast and loose with reality? Sure. Do I care? Not particularly. This is, as they say, my show after all.

Hit me with a fresh chapter.

AR Bennett

Track 3: Deep Fantasy

Gone are the board shorts and band tee. Same goes for the flip-flops and the cheap knockoff Ray-Bans. Hell gone is the beach house and all of the shoddy furniture and sandy floors. Gone too is the beach even. In its place there's the interior of a white shipping van. You know the type. Probably most definitely a Dodge. Sort of looks like some short eyes would be offering kids sweats out of the back of it. And sitting behind the driver seat there's Bones. He's got mirrored aviator sunglasses on that cover most of his face and his blonde mess of curly hair is kept under control by a black knit hat.

The van comes to a stop at the red light reflecting in Bones's shades. He turns in his seat and holds up three fingers. "Three minutes."

From the back cargo area of the van, I nod my head and repeat the countdown to Alaska and Scooby, both of which are tightly packed on a bench across from me. Simultaneously we start getting ready. Pulling on black latex gloves before tugging black Kevlar vests over our matching business suits that you better believe are black as well. Call it Reservoir Dogs chic. The van moves through an intersection and Bones holds up two fingers.

It's getting real now.

My watch ticks and tocks in hyper stylized fashion. Each tick pronounced and each tock picking up the deep bass tones of Dolby Digital. I nod to my dudes sitting across from me. Face hardened and ready. Calm as Hindu cows. From the top of my head, I pull down a rubber mask that looks like someone in Indonesia tried to recreate JFK from memory. Similarly, Alaska and Scooby pull down masks that are these same almost passable impressions of Richard Nixon and LBJ respectively. Up front Bones pulls down his hat so that it becomes something similar to a balaclava.

The van accelerates.

Here we go.

With the deft touch of a Formula 1 driver Bones yanks the wheel and cuts across two lanes of traffic. Horns blare. Tires skid. He drives the van up on the curb and next thing you know he's yelling

"Go Go GO GO!"

The sliding door of the back of the van flings open and the three of us in the back jump out. I've got a chrome plated Desert Eagle in my grip while Scooby wields a sawed-off pump shotgun with a pistol grip. Alaska, true to form, is carrying the biggest gun you've ever seen. Belt fed. About as long as one of the big man's beefy arms. Something that would be right at home hanging off the side of a Black Hawk doing donuts over a war-torn neighborhood in Somalia.

In front of us there's a blocky building made of white Italian marble and finely polished glass. It screams posh. People on the sidewalk dive out of the way as the realization of what is happening sets in. With purpose and a calm that is commanding I stride to the front of the building and kick open the glass doors.

"Nobody move!" I'm shouting. People are letting out startled gasps and shocked cries. A thick guard with powdered donut sugar speckled on his lapel catches my eye. Puts his hand on the butt of his six-shooter. I turn and face him, showing off the hand cannon in my grip. I can see his eyes scan over the piece. Taking it all in. He seems to mouth out each letter as he reads the branding.

D E S E R T E A G L E . 5 0

"No need to be a hero today man." I command. The guard nods and follows the barrel of my gun's instructions to lay down on his ample belly on the floor. "Good. Now slowly slide out your piece and push it my way."

He does. Alaska and Scooby control the rest of the crowd. Getting them to lay down same as the rent-a-cop had before them. Soon the marble floor is lined with prone bodies whimpering into their arms and hiding their faces from the men in masks with guns.

"Okay. Now this isn't your money. This is the bank's money…"

Nixon coughs at me and gives me this sort of hands up shrug that is fairly widely accepted as the universal gesture for "what the hell man?".

"…errr…this is the club's money. Property. Whatever not important. What is important is that your property is ensured by the federal government and you won't be losing a dime. So nothing worth giving your life over."

"Cops are on their way." Comes Bones's voice in my ear. It is tingling with static and electrical interference from the earbud. "We gotta move."

I make my way to the counter where a blonde in a skimpy bank teller's uniform is leaning. "Hey there doll. They let you come to work in that?"

Watson looks down at the outfit and shrugs. "You picked it."

"I do have to say I didn't know this about me until now but this whole bank robber / bank teller vibe is sorta working for me."

She laughs. "Well, I've got handcuffs if you want to take em for a spin?"

"Really?"

"Jesus Christ. Focus" Nixon snaps. He's covering a group of people that are looking pretty antsy. Tensions are indeed high.

"Yeah yeah." I motion for Watson to grab the key off the manager's belt and she makes her way to the vault door. Things are going very well. My watch's tempo is right on cue.

Watson uses the key to open the lock and the giant steel door comes open with a pressurized hiss. The stacks of gold inside sparkle in the sunlight and I can't stop from grinning under my mask.

The smile lasts just up until the first shot rings out.

Crack.

No more smile.

Bones is yelling in my ear. 'They're on us. They're on us man. Get to the van! Get. To. The. Van!"

Sniper bullets begin streaming in from the windows. Helicopter spotlights cast brilliant circles of light on the floor. There's another crack. Alaska stumbles a few steps as the round planks of his armored vest. Growling rage and spitting hot anger he spins the belt fed up and starts laying down cover fire.

Boom boom boom boom

Everyone is yelling now.

Scoob goes down. He's hit! I rush up and grab him by his vest. Watson is stuffing gold bars into bags at her feet. "We gotta go! We're surrounded!"

Boomboomboomboom

Heavy machine gun fire echoes through the confined space deafing all the other chaos and noise. Suddenly the glass front of the building explodes inwards and men in tactical gear come flying in on ropes from the roof.

AR Bennett

Goddamnit if I'm not going to take a few of these bastards with me. I raise my gun and

"Okay enough."

*****

The glossy film quality covering the setting evaporates bringing the KBH back to its worn and faded life. Alaska and Bones are on their feet chanting GET TO THE VAN. A regular barfly has stumbled off his stool and is covering our retreat with a mop cradled in his arms like a M16 straight outa Nam.

How's that for a slice of fried gold?

It takes me a moment to realize I am standing on one of the bar tables that probably shouldn't be stood on. The table leg groans precariously in protest. I dismount in a way that garners 10s across the board except for the Russian judge who gives it an 8.5.

"You're an idiot." Scooby eyes me in a way that tells me he probably really does mean it.

"Oh, come on. Don't tell me that didn't move something in you Scoob." I say as I grab an offered beer and pop the top chipping yet another scratch into the wood of the bar. "Thought it was pretty damn good myself."

"So, your entire plan is to basically to a shot for shot remake of 'Heat'?" He asks.

"They call it a classic for a reason, Scoob."

"You know they all get shot right? It doesn't go well for them."

Yeah. Obliviously. But then again, what can I say? Give me a good and proper bad guy. The look. The tone. The way they deal with situations. Born on the outs and out of pocket but soaking up all that sweet sweet limelight. You idolize anything enough and you become it. Manifest Destiny for an impressionable mind. None of these "movies make kids violent" thoughts though. There's no time for your pearl clutching nonsense if you swallow that pill without making a sour face. Movies don't make kids want to be violent.

Movies make kids want to become gangsters.

And if nothing else, The Bad Bunch has a bit of that in us.

Just look around.

The walls are adorned with eclectic memorabilia including but not limited to a shocking number of framed mugshots. Some of which are fairly recent while others are dated to the way way back.

I'm up there. So is Scoob. So is Alaska. So is almost everyone else who even casually associates with The Bunch. Bones has a newer one not yet crinkled and yellowed with age. In fact, the only one to not have a spot of honor on the Wall of Fame is Watson, but then she's always had a knack for getting out of trouble, now hasn't she?

"Yeah, we aren't doing that. You still haven't presented an actual plan for your plan." Scooby states finally.

"I mean, if you don't want to go the classic way then it's super easy." I shrug. "Bones flies us in low and dark. We repel out of the helo in the dead of night. Alaska takes out the guards Delta Force style. You drill the safe for me to secure the goods. Then it's Miller Time. Easy Peasy lemon."

"You…you do know we live in reality, right?"

I sip my beer and hold Scooby's stare. His bushy eyebrow is arched in silent question and perhaps not so silent accusation. After a lifetime together we have mastered the art of non-verbal communication. Finally, Scoob sighs and shakes his head.

"This isn't a movie Saint." He states. "What you're talking about is breaking and entering into a respected place in the community that has maintained its respect and privacy by taking security seriously."

"It's a yacht club Scoob. We wouldn't be breaking into Fort Knox here man."

"Why are we breaking into anything at all?"

Scooby knows why. He knows more about our business than anyone, especially when it comes to our books. Books that have been looking rather thin as of late. I don't really feel the need to tell him why, but I will tell you. Keep it our little secret yeah?

Why are we doing this? The Plan? Because Brandon Lake wrote an album that's why. Not just any album. The punk rock community's equivalent to the Holy Grail. The lost - and presumably last - album of Lake Effect in Affect. Rumored to contain groundbreaking tracks that push the boundaries and redefine the scene. Those in the know know this is something truly special. Innovative. Raw. And even more importantly…

Worth a fortune.

Album sales of rockstars go up many percent when those rockstars become dead rockstars. Funny how that happens. Art only getting value when the artist is no longer there to reap the rewards. Sort of sad actually. That said, while I would love to appreciate - artistically speaking - the punk world's Shangri La for what it is, we sort of need it for what it could be. That is to say

A paycheck.

The way I see it this potential masterpiece belongs to us anyways. See before platinum artist, punk rocker boy, and personal friend Brandon Lake up and found himself missing presumed dead enough to be declared dead, he was a frequent visitor of the Kelso Beach House - yep complete with his own mugshot on the wall and all - and he would spend his time here working on his craft. In between shooting up and getting smacked out of course. That made it ours by default. Possession being 9/10th of the law or whatever. I'm no lawyer clearly, but that feels like it would hold up in court.

So, all we have to do is get the damn thing.

"Look, none of this is that hard. We know where the album is, we know the layout of where the album is, we just have to go get it."

"How's it we know where it is?"

Because it's not really that hard to figure out. This isn't exactly Sherlock Holmes shit here. Brandon Lake, when not on tour, lived almost exclusively in three places: his apartment downtown, his yacht, and here. The apartment has since been condemned and it's not like there is an album just laying around the place here, sooo…

"It's on Brando's ship."

"Boat." Scooby has his arms crossed over his bony chest again and is standing his ground. "It's a boat not a ship."

"What's the difference?"

"Do you really want me to explain it?" Scoob sighs. If sighs could be stylized in font this one would be exasperated and oddly enough italic. If he really wanted to explain it he could. Scooby has done odd work at the yacht club in question after all. If there is anyone in the Bunch that knows the difference between boats and ships it would be him.

But now it just feels like we're arguing over semantics.

"Not particularly. But it's like I said this album is on Brando's boat and all we have to do is go get it."

"The boat in the yacht club?"

"Correct."

"The boat in the yacht club that is surrounded by guards?"

Now it's my turn to sigh. I throw my hands up in the air before giving the rest of The Bunch a look like help me out here boys. Alaska simply shrugs as if to say "I said I could handle it".

"Look if you don't want Alaska to do his thing then - I dunno - Watson will just seduce them."

"All of them?"

I look at Watson, my blue eyes meeting hers inquisitively. "Yes?"

"Sure." She states flatly and then emphasizes the point with a mix of an indifferent head nod and a confident shrug. "Not a problem."

"Really?" Scooby and I say simultaneously though for entirely different reasons. Watson laughs softly and shakes her head.

"Yea I'm game why not."

"All of them huh…really…wow…all three. Yea umm..hmm." It is not often I find myself at a loss for words. Words sort of being my thing and all. "Would three be a problem, I dunno, say…here?"

I feel like it is fair of me to want to have follow up questions. Questions that no longer involve albums and yachts and yacht clubs with guards or any of the other businesses of the day. Watson doesn't blush, hell she doesn't even blink, she just keeps my gaze with a mischievous look sparkling in her green eyes.

"Depends on the three." She says finally.

"Well, me of course."

"Of course." She nods in agreement.

"And then you pick the third. Though I could make suggestions. Bones for example is out, obviously. This isn't West Virginia. But I mean other than that world's your oyster. Rob's Sister. Jenny From the Block. Peanut Butter Pauline…"

"How about," Watson says after a soft nibble of her bottom lip. "Alaska."

"Alaska?!"

Don't love that.

Especially the way she said it. Cool. Calm. As if we were discussing the weather coming over the lake, or a back page article in the sports section of the Times. Quick too. How would that even work? It's not a matter of will, it's simple geometry. A logistical issue stemming squarely around physics. Watson is short and slender with her slenderness accented by curves in all the right places. But she is short. I'm not saying it's impossible. I'm just having a hard time wrapping my brain around it, that's all. Then there is the issue of where I'd fit in…

"How does your brain work?" Scooby asks, breaking up that potentially disturbing train of thought. And thank goodness too because I'm not sure I was fully prepared for it to arrive at the station.

"Opportunistically." I state bringing the conversation back on course. "Which is why we are doing the Lake Job and sticking to my plan."

The Lake Job? Whoa, settle down there Danny Ocean.

As far as plans go this one seems pretty solid. To me. To Scooby probably not so much because he still isn't convinced. He throws his hands up in the air. Pulls at his beard. Huffs. Puffs. Comes just short of kicking an empty chair, thinks better of putting it out of place, and ultimately sits down and pours a drink "We don't need this right now Saint. We've got the Canadian thing going and that's going well. All of this is just distraction."

AR Bennett

The Canadian Thing.

There is that. Here's the thing about The Canadian Thing. When people - especially Americans - think of product being moved over a border they tend to think South to North. That's what dominates the news anyways. But things also need moving the other way around. North to South. The Canadian Thing is the closest any of us lovable degenerates will ever come to having a 9-5.

By bringing up our "day jobs" Scooby is essentially playing his Ace in the hole. Good for him, I'll give credit where credit is due. That's a smart move on his part. And he knows it. Just look at that smug face.

Except…

Except I've got one better.

"One," I say slowly to emphasize each and every syllable. "Point. Five."

If any one of the Bunch had not been paying particular attention before they are now. 1.5. Just a string of numbers sure, unless you've been in the game for a bit. Then it is a whole different ball of wax. No one ever says "one point anything" if they are talking about hundreds.

Or thousands for that matter.

One Point Five. As In: A heap. A packet. A pile. The full ten yards. Fat stacks and big racks. Bands on bands.

One Million. Five-hundred thousand. Dollars.

"American?" Bones whistles in disbelief.

"No Scandinavian." I snap sarcastically. "Yes. American."

"For that amount of scratch, I'd seduce the guards myself." Bones laughs. Alaska nods his big head in agreement. Even Watson is taken back slightly.

"No buyer will pay that much for something no one is sure even exists."

"The one I found will. See Scoob," I hold up a finger and let the pause be filled with the ever-present sounds of construction noise. "Inevitability. And nothing gums up the wheels of progress faster than bureaucracy other than a very full bag. So, we're doing this. We just have to decide if we are doing it soft or loud. Thems the options."

The room is silent for a moment as everyone lets my words sink in. But it is not silent for long.

"How about another way?" Watson asks politely.

"What other way?" Scooby and I say in unison.

AR Bennett

Track Four: Enama of The State

Watson's other way it turned out didn't involve guards, guns, or seduction even.

But it did sadly involve another suit.

I have to give credit where credit is due, Watson came up with a pretty solid plan all things considered. Which is odd. Not because Watson isn't smart - she is - but because historically she is not the one to come up with the plans. She has always up until this point preferred a more hands off approach to The Bunch's shenanigans, usually waiting in reserve until things have already played out then stepping in if things hit the fan.

But here she is. The star-spangled woman with a plan.

Not for the first time I'm getting this vibe that there are things Watson's not telling me. Secrets are a way of life in this life, sure. We all got 'em. Everyone keeps things in the dark and tries desperately to do our best to not allow them to spill out onto the front page. The only difference is

I know the rest of the Bunch's secrets.

And while she has helped us out of a few jams and jellies over the last few months if/when our capers go awry, this would be the first time she has proposed to help plan one. Part of me wants to believe she is just getting more involved, stepping up to the plate as it were. Then there's the other part.

Wouldn't be the first time I fell for some skirt and flirt and ended up down a road I didn't want to go. Hell, probably wouldn't be the last.

"Penny for your thoughts?"

She's got her head on my shoulder and my arm around her waist as we walk. Even without looking up to see my face she can sense the hamster wheel in my head spinning. No surprise there. Intuition is another one of her traits.

"I'll give you a million pennies when we pull this off." I say finally with a smile. Play off my hesitation as simply being uncomfortable in this monkey suit.

"You do know that's not how pennies work right?" She laughs. Her breath is hot on my ear and the way her lips touch my skin softly makes me smile more. She pulls her lips back and lifts her head up to look me in the eyes. "Seriously though Saint, what's on your mind?"

"Just thinking maybe you'd rather have had Alaska as your date."

This of course is not technically a lie. Call it more of an omission. I am thinking that…only that's just one thought amongst other things. Watson studies my face with a clinical gaze that would make even the most professional poker players squirm a bit. Luckily for me I am genetically predisposed to duplicity.

"Jealousy doesn't look good on you Saint." She states firmly and finally before her features soften a tad and the corners of her mouth twitch up. She rubs her hand down my back before giving my butt a soft pat. "But this suit sure does. Besides, I couldn't have taken Alaska. Not with you sending him off on 'other business'."

"Gotta keep 'em separated." I laugh and give her a wink. "Don't want to have to fight my biggest friend over my girl ya know?"

"I'm your girl now then?"

Well, no need to go and put a label on it or anything. I just nod and give her a quick kiss on the cheek. The summer air is warm with a refreshing breeze coming up and off the lake. I run my fingers down her skin which I gotta admit is the nicest feature of a dress with no back. We continue to walk down the street with only the large flat moon occasionally poking through the overhead trees to guide us to our destination.

Though the word "street" is a bit of a disservice.

While it is technically a road - as in: it is paved, straight, and cars drive on it - this street is actually labeled as a boulevard. Not because it is bisected down the middle, but because the word boulevard conjures up images of Hollywood and Vine. 90210. A street can be any backwater bit of asphalt. A boulevard? Now that's fine class and high to do. As we walk, Watson's heels and these ridiculous leather loafers I've been forced into click and clack briskly on the smoothest pavement this cracked and crumbling city has ever seen. Only the sound doesn't travel far before fading into silence as it gets lost in a canopy of thick manicured vegetation.

I'm no botanist or tree specialist but to my untrained eye the trees lining this street that isn't a street look like oak. Which makes sense. We're heading to a yacht club after all.

Lake Erie freezes. Occasionally almost solid. So, whatever goes on here only needs to be kept hidden during the months when the water of the bay is still, you know, water and yachts can sail on it. Hence the oak trees. Had this place been open year-round I'm sure the founders would have probably planted pine. But big thick trees that sprout in the spring and summer and then block the winds and snow off the road in the fall and winter would suffice. A man-made forest that keeps intruders and Looky Lou's out like a natural leafy fence. Then there's the actual fence.

The respected Lake Erie Yacht Club is a member only club that maintains its privacy in a few ways. First, the tree shrouded street we're currently walking down is so hidden you wouldn't know it was there if you hadn't been looking for it. There is no sign on the nearest connecting road. No adverts or indicators. Just a small metal plaque on a metal pole that reads "Private". Going unnoticed will only get you so far if you are looking to keep a place secure. Beyond that you'll need actual you know…security. That's where the fence comes in.

Wrought iron poles pushed down into a few feet of concrete. While designed to look decorative, those decorations are actually dangerous. Look closely enough and you'll see the Fluer-de-lis styled post caps are actually rather sharp with the pointy bits being particularly pointy. The fence wraps its way around the place using the hilly terrain and the steep cliffs the club is nestled down into as natural advantages. The only way in or out is a gated entrance that is guarded by wouldn't you know it: guards.

A lot has gone into keeping this private club private.

Hidden street. Sharp and secure fence. Hostile landscaping. Guards. Everything comes together with one singular purpose and that's to keep undesirable riff raff out.

Which makes being an undesirable riff raff getting in all the more fun.

Especially if the way I got in is by invitation and not aquatic invasion.

"You sure they'll just let us in?" I ask quietly as we approach the guard station.

Watson laughs and nods. "That's how invites work Saint."

She rummages through her discrete clutch and withdraws two embossed invites. I smile at the guards as they check them. They don't smile back and as much as I hate to admit Scooby was right. I can see the butt of holstered pistols under tight suit jackets as they wave us in.

Well let's call it partially right.

Yes, the guards do indeed have guns. However, there are a hell of a lot more of them than just three. Like a lot more. Knowing an exact count and placement could come in handy for what I'm about to do, so I start counting them in my head. It's around fifteen that I give up and just go under the assumption that when it comes to the guards' numbers, they have enough of them.

Of course, if everything comes up Aces with Watson's plan, I might not even have to muck about with these jelly donut munchers. Still…seems like an awful lot for some boats.

"These sorts of shindigs usually come with this level of security?"

"Sometimes." Watson nods. She may have her head on my shoulder again but I can tell she too is playing the counting guard's game. "Depends on who all is invited."

"So, what we got the mayor and the queen of England or something?"

"Probably not her majesty. Not tonight anyways."

"Seriously?" I think she's kidding but when her eyes say she isn't I let out a slow stunned whistle. "How'd you even get an invite to something like this anyways?"

"My family and the Colt Foundation go back. Play at the same clubs." She shrugs nonchalantly. "That sort of thing."

THE BAD BUNCH 41

There are a great many clubs dotted about this quiet corner of Northwestern Pennsylvania. Clubs for people with German heritage or Italian heritage or those for whom trace their lines back to the Holy Roman Empire. Britannia. Constantinople. Reading Clubs and Bridge Clubs. Clubs where members call their leader The Grand Poopon. There is even a club where you pay $20 on a bi-monthly basis so that you can pay $7 – the cheapest in the city – for a full prime rib dinner with all the fixings. This town loves a club.

But I suspect Watson isn't talking about those sorts of clubs.

Those aren't the sort of clubs people with connections to the Foundation migrate to. Instead, those sorts of folks stick to golf clubs, tennis clubs, and yes even yacht clubs. Clubs with fences and hedges and all the rest. Private clubs.

The Colt Foundation.

Ugh.

If you've ever gotten blackout drunk off of raspberry schnapps in college to the point that the ensuing violent vomiting has prevented you from even being able to smell artificial raspberries ever again, you'll understand the logic of why that name puts a bad taste in my mouth.

Some experiences just leave a lingering effect.

The Foundation is the public and supposedly benevolent arm of Colt Industries which itself is the corporate arm of one real estate tycoon and sustained pain in my ass

Barnaby J. Colt.

The Mistake on The Lake's very own monarch incarnate.

If you were to boil down the city of Erie into one analogy you could do a lot worse than a corrupt pound full of naughty dogs. Barking. Yipping.

Tearing up the furniture. You get the idea. If that's the case then Colt is dog number one.

A millionaire a few times over and then a few times over that. The top 1% of the one percent. That fact alone would make him dangerous on any given Sunday, but what is the real kicker is that he's a bit more one of us in him than even he'd like to admit. We're not exactly cut from the same cloth but we're in the same sweatshop if you get my drift.

See, Colt came up the hard way. A whole bunch of shady little deals that grew into shady big deals. Fleabag motels and laundromats that became bars on the main strip and hotels on the water. Restaurants. Coffee shops. Shopping malls. Strip Clubs, Golf Clubs, and as it turns out Yacht Clubs.

Colt owns the whole damn town.

Lucky for me Kelso Beach isn't in town. Not yet. Not officially anyways. But those condo McMansions that keep being built up and down my beach? Those aren't being built by themselves, now are they? Someone has a hand on the wheel of "progress", and that someone just so happens to be the very person whose party I'm about to crash.

"You couldn't have ties with any other sleazeball who slips a boat here? Anyone at all? It had to be him." I ask Watson. We are walking toward what can only be described as a gilded floating affront to both good taste and God.

"Only one I could get on short notice. You're the one who said you needed to get to Brandon's yacht sooner rather than later." She responds. "This is sooner."

I get it. Beggars can't be choosers and all that. The thing about fancy boats is that they are a bit like birds of a feather, they dock together. If Brandon Lake's lost album is on Brandon Lake's boat, then I've got to go to where Brandon's boat is.

That's the hope anyways.

I'm not a big fan of living on a hope and a prayer. Shocking for a guy named Saint I know. But I'd very much rather have my destiny in my own hands thank you very much. Which is why that "other business" Alaska is on is my way of hedging my bets.

Brando lived in three places remember?

I think I skipped that part for the sake of moving the plot along, but as I'm not particularly eager to step on Colt's big fat floating phallus we can use this opportunity for a bit of a flashback. I'll have a smoke and enjoy the summer air here until you get back.

*****

I swim out past the breakers and dunk my head under the warm water. When I come up Watson is there and I pull her in close. She kisses my neck as the soft waves float us about. Lazily my fingers work to untie the straps of her bikini. She leans in close and nibbles at my ear.

"You sure you want an audience for this?" She whispers seductively.

"Nope. This is for us. Just went a little too far back is all."

With a snap of my fingers the dark waters brighten by the rays of a brand-new day, complete with construction noise and all. To the probable dismay of all those coming here with hopes of spice and loin girdling titillation, the romantic beach setting shifts back into the grimy and gritty beach house that I call home. In the industry it's called a 'Smash Cut'.

"If you're so sure this album or whatever is on Brandon's boat why do Bones and I got to schlep it over to downtown?" Alaska asks. He's got his big arms crossed his big chest.

There we go. Now we're at where we should be.

"Because like I literally just said I don't want to bet our fortunes on a hope and a prayer." I've pulled him and Bones aside under the guise of getting more beer. We're in the kitchen of the KBH away from prying ears.

'When did you say that?" Bones asks. There is confusion written all over his face as he racks his brain trying to remember when I said the thing that I just said I said. Flashback humor is not for everyone it turns out.

"That's not important right now. What is important is I need you two to go and scope out Brando's pad. Cover all our bases."

Alaska and Bones nod in agreement, though Bones is looking none too pleased about it.

"Is that a problem?"

"It's just that…well that place is scuzzy bro. Noone but a junky wants to be spending time at the Junky's Boneyard now do they?"

"Wear gloves."

"Okayyy. Do you own any gloves?"

"I rent to own Bones." I say between pinching the bridge of my nose. That swim you all played peepshow on was supposed to cure my hangover, but the last few conversations have been putting those healing properties to work. The headache is nearly back in full force. "Just make it work."

"Scoob's not going to be happy." Alaska states flatly and Bones nods his head in agreement. "We're supposed to be running defensive linemen for the Canadians."

"Let me handle Scooby."

"What's going on with you two? You two not vibing on this new job?"

"Mommy and daddy aren't getting a divorce if that's what you're asking. Just do this thing for me will ya? I'll take care of the rest."

"So, you get to go to a fancy party and we get shipped out to hepatitis alley?" Bones whines. "Doesn't seem fair."

"Trust me you're getting the better end of the stick bro." I crack one of the beers and take a long pull. "At least the junkies don't want you dead."

Probably

*****

I flick my cigarette into the black waters near some trust fund kid's catamaran. Watson looks at me expectedly before giving me a shall we get going type gesture. She taps a heel impatiently. I'm not seeing what the rush is. From the sounds of things this party is barely getting started anyways. Or maybe that's just how rich people's parties' sound.

To emphasis this a string quartet strikes up and the soft music float across the dock.

Definitely not how we do it in my neck of the woods.

"Into the belly of the beast we go."

"You never know you might actually enjoy yourself." Watson laughs and pulls on my suit sleeve to get me moving. "If nothing else you'll at least know the booze will be good."

"Now that I can get behind." I laugh.

AR Bennett

Track Five: Sorry Ma, Forgot To Take Out The Trash

The way the party started was far less memorable than how it ended.

Here's the thing about the lifestyles of small town rich and famous, especially the lifestyles of old rich and famous, turns out the lifestyle is boring as shit.

Golf talk. Boat talk. Talk about golfing off of boats. 401Ks and IRAs. Sandals with socks yes, or no? It's all sweaters and shrimp cocktails on silver platters between scotches and stogies. A few ounces of giddy up and some dancers of the fabricless variety would have done wonders for this shindig.

A nice summer night like this there would be more brass happening on the back porch of the KBH than an orchestra. I don't provide the stuff. I'm not in the cartel game. But I'm a strong believer that the customer is always right. Who am I to stop their good times?

Let's just call the Kelso Beach House B.Y.O.C and leave it at that.

Bring Your Own Columbian.

If the cops on the beat and detectives on the street are close enough to see my customers hitting the slopes before hitting the beach we're already in big enough trouble as it is.

So, I let it slide.

That said I'd wished I had a few goes at the old nose candy prior to getting here. This just isn't my scene. The dog and pony show. Being here to say that you were here. It's disingenuous. The hangers-on that flock to these sorts of soirees so they can name drop it later in some other boring conversation between boring people.

This isn't a party.

It's a goddamn political arms race.

It is pomp and circumstance.

That's Colt's whole thing. Come. Have a drink. Use a bedroom to bang someone other than your wife. But know this: If someone more important than you come about, someone more interesting or more connected, this is all going to be used for my benefit.

Call me old fashioned but I believe connection should be about connecting not connections. There are more important things than the web woven between who you know and how you know them. My people are my people. Not because they are useful to me, but because they are my people.

This?

Whatever this is?

It's all so fake it is funny.

It's fancy fugazi. Meant to impress and win closed door dick measuring contests. Even Colt's ridiculous yacht is just that. A hundred-foot dildo that dominates the thousand odd other boats docked about here. Everything is polished brass and deep mahogany. Rich leathers and cigar smoke. Don't let the ultra-flat screens fool you. This boat is meant to transport you to another time.

His.

Good scotch though. Probably as old as most of the guests milling about. I let the smokey taste roll on the back of my tongue and down my throat as I try to blend in as best as I can. Which is much harder than it seems. To me getting "dressed" up is either a gray linen suit for weddings - and now yacht parties - or a black suit for funerals. Compared to everyone else on deck I might as well be wearing sweatpants and a hoodie with POOR stenciled in big block letters across my chest.

Even the waitstaff are wearing tuxedos.

Luckily most eyes aren't on me. A woman like Watson in a dress like that will have that effect, doubly so if most of the eyes about the place are in the skulls of dirty old men jacked to the man tits on Cialis. Next to her I might as well be a bit of deck furniture. Which suits me just fine.

I trace my fingers down her bare back and she flutters. Dresses like the one she's wearing are made for that sort of thing. She smiles and cuddles close against the cool breeze coming off the lake. This summer has been a swelter so far. Hot and bone dry. Even the lake is shallow, the boats sitting low against the docks. Still any breeze that comes from Canada could be considered chilly. Especially, I'd imagine, in a dress with no back.

"It's a shame you've got a job to do." She pines.

"Hey," I laugh trying very *very* hard to not get well…just that. "This was your idea. I opted for a full-frontal assault. You're the one who wanted to go in all James Bond like."

"What if it was just a date? Would that be so terrible? You and me, some scotch, some slow dancing. Wouldn't you want that?"

It feels like there is bait on the end of this hook. I pull away from our embrace and look down at her. "What's on your mind?"

The band – and who even has a live band these days – strikes up a soft melody. It's a full set of strings. Violin. Cello. The works. Here too the band members are in black tuxedos, which to me makes their playing all the more impressive. I'm uncomfortable in a linen suit and I'm not weighted down but a four-foot wood instrument. God knows what it's like in tux. I don't normally go in for the classics, but you can tell the band is passionate about their craft and I can appreciate that.

Watson sips her scotch and watches me over the rim of her glass. I suddenly feel like I'm being studied. There is a clinical nature to her look. Like a teacher grading a test or a scientist with a slide under a microscope. Something seems to have her interest.

"Do you ever think about getting out of this life? Settling down?" She asks finally.

"Why?"

She hesitates. Chews through a thought in her head and seems to weigh whether or not it is worth saying out loud. Finally with a manicured finger she points subtly over my shoulder towards the yacht's stateroom where a group of men smoking cigars have gathered. I look without looking. A skill this life has taught me.

"You see that guy over there by the bar with the trophy wife at his side barely hanging on each word?"

"The guy with the bad rug on his head?"

"No, the other one next to him."

"Well, he's got quite the hairpiece too. I don't think more than ten people, not including us, the staff, or the band, have their real hair."

She pinches my side a bit more sharply than playful. This is a stop messing about and listen gesture. She's clearly got something she wants to tell me. Not messing about has historically not been one of my strong suits, but I try my best.

"What about him?"

"He's the police commissioner for the EPD."

AR Bennett

She likes to remind people that she is connected. That she has prospects and that she is only down in the sand with the bad ones because she chooses to be. This however, doesn't feel like that.

"And the guy next to him is the chief editor of the Erie Tribune. The guy next to him is a judge."

Watson goes down the list of the who is who mingling about the party. It's a veritable meet and greet of heavy hitting and powerful people. The inner cabal. This small town's very own Illuminati. I'm not getting the feeling she is pointing names and naming fingers just to show off. There is something else lurking behind her controlled expression.

I just can't see it.

"Colt has influential friends. Makes sense he's an influential guy." I say with a shrug when she has finished. "So what?"

"You know most of the people in this room have files on you." It's not a question so much as it is a statement. "A lot of these people want to see you go down Saint."

We're held close and whispering like conspirators which you could say we actually are. Conspiring. She's whispering in my ear, keeping her face tucked in about my neck so to snuggle against the wind. Or to give any knowing eyes less chance of recognition. Still, I like being close to her. Even in the calm shallow waters there is some soft chop. Light waves brush against the side of the hull like my fingers brush against skin. We ride the slight sway together. On our own private little surf session.

I like being close to people.

I've never gone half in a day in my life. More of an all or nothing sort of guy. As much as I can. All the time. Always. You know what they say about the brightest candles?

As far as I can tell she likes being close to me because I'm a bit of the bad life. The other side of the tracks. Tramps and ladies. Songs as old as rhymes. An opportunity to see what life is like down in the shade of ivory towers. A bit of the bad life boy toy.

But not too bad.

Surely not bad enough to merit files thick with intelligence from some of the real bad power brokers this rotten little city is made up by. But she's saying that I need to be serious. Focus. Pay attention because this will be on the test.

It's just that that's not really my style. I try and break this new found tension with a bit of humor.

"When you say files do you mean big files?" I can practically feel her rolling her eyes. She knows where this is going. "Large and thick and girthy files?"

"Be serious for a second Saint."

Gone is any semblance of the flirty tone. Gone too is the playful attitude. The way she said it and the way her eyes look deep into mine? That felt like a warning.

Here's the thing I've never learned about holes though. When I'm in one I've never really learned how to stop digging.

"What can I say? I've got more papers than the KGB. I'm an interesting guy. Isn't that why you like me?"

"I do like you." I can tell there's an ask coming. Something she wants to sell me on. "What about we just forget about this tape? Just walk away from this whole thing. Go have that smoke and swim and enjoy the night on Kelso Beach. Just go have a night. You and me."

"It's a bit too late for that aint it?"

"It doesn't have to be. The night's still young. The scotch is good. Let's just leave it at that."

Now it's my turn to give her a quizzical look. For as long as I've known her, which is less than the rest of The Bunch, I've never known her to be skittish. Everything so far is going according to plan. If I turn my head I can see Brandon's boat from here. It's just right there.

"I guess…" She starts softly. This is the whisper of conflict. Of things that maybe need to be said but then again maybe not. "I guess what if this doesn't go how you plan Saint? What then?"

"Then I'll make a new plan."

Watson sighs and shakes her head. Blonde strands of hair fall out onto your face and I brush it back behind her ear. "It's what I do."

"Yeah…it's what you do." She looks up at me and for a moment there's something that should have been said between us but wasn't. She untangles herself from me and steps back. She's smiling but I can see storm clouds darkening her eyes. Just for a flash. Then it's gone and her expression and posture are back to the Watson I know. "Don't you have an album to go and get?"

I nod. That's the plan after all. Isn't it?

She takes my drink out of my hands, fingers lingering on mine for a few heart beats before setting it on the bar table. As covert as I can be I roll my slacks up to my ankles and slide out of the leather loafers and socks. She slides them discreetly under some deck furniture.

This party is a fairly packed affair. Lot of eyes. But that doesn't mean that those eyes are all looking at us. Most people are here to only focus on themselves. I lean over the railing of the deck and quickly start judging distances. I was never good at math. Mostly because I never showed up for math class, but I have an eye for angles. Geometry and physics can be powerful tools. I've had to learn both the hard way.

There's no school like the school of hard knocks. Each and every one of my scars is a testament to that fact.

I play out what I'm about to do in my head.

It's a bit of a drop from the deck down to the boat adjacent and below. Nothing I can't handle. Though, if I did mess it up and everything goes wrong in a hurry, I would be hoping for more open space to fall into. With this heat wave the lake is slowly draining. Still, it's enough to keep the boats afloat and moving with the current. If I bungle this drop, I'd be wedged between two very heavy and unyielding masses, one wrong wave and I would find myself as paste on the hull of either.

The first drop is by and far the biggest, once I clear that there is a row of smaller yachts that spans to the north. It might be a bit of action movie but I shouldn't have a problem crossing from one to another by going from deck to deck to deck until I've landed on the one I need. Which is naturally the last one.

Because of course it is.

From there I just need to keep a keen eye on the dark shadows. Hate to trip over loose rope and end up with another broken bone or two. Or worse yet in the drink.

Watson seems to really like this suit. Hate to mess it up.

Broken bones I can handle. Suit shopping, I simply cannot.

I take one last gulp of scotch to steady my nerves. One last look around for prying eyes. Then I roll my neck until it pops satisfyingly. Rotate my shoulders to relieve the jittery tension building there. Knuckles crack bone. Softly bouncing from one foot to the other. This is a pre-game ritual I am very familiar with.

There are a great many drugs in this world of ours. Countless ways to get and stay high. No matter what you snort, sniff, smoke, or shoot up, nothing comes close to the feeling of doing a bit of the bad thing. Gearing up to do something against the rules, against the norm, counter to the culture and outside the law. Dopamine receptors flare up. Serotonin releases. Adrenaline flows. Pupils dilate. Breath quickens. The nervous system comes alive with crackles of bio-energy bringing the world into ultra-HD clarity.

Nothing beats a micro-dose of crime to get the blood flowing.

I let the nerves wash over me like tides over sand. Can you feel that? That electric energy that crackles to life making sure to let you know you're alive. That right there is the good stuff. That's what this life is all about.

Are you ready?

"As I'll ever be."

Watson looks confused. It's not like she can hear my inner monologue. "What?"

"Nothing." I smile. "Be right back."

"I'll be here waiting. Eagerly."

"In that case I better hurry." A kiss on the cheek. A smirk. A wink.

And I'm off. Into the night.

Track Six: Fresh Fruit For Rotting Vegetables

This scene is basically made for the movies. The cover of darkness. Guests and guards in their black tie best. The cocky and – if I do say so myself – incredibly charming hero dashing off to do some vaguely implausible acrobatics without breaking a sweat. This is pure uncut grade A silver screen pulp.

James Bond.

Ethan Hunt.

Jason Bourne.

You tell me that if you were faced with breaking into a guarded facility under false pretense, infiltrating a yacht party of high-ranking community officials and their wannabe gangster host, only to slip off the side and Splinter Cell stealth your way to a secret safe holding valuable and confidential documents that you wouldn't feel at least a little bit cinema spy like. Eight-year-old me would be going nuts.

Hell yeah little bro! Look at us now!

Now all we got to do is bust out some sick moves and karate chop our way through some goons. Laser watch our way into a locked door. Blast a bunch of henchmen with a silenced pistol. Pop. Headshot. Pop pop. Headshot headshot. We're so fucking cool right now.

Sweet dreams are made of these.

As often is the case when faced with actually doing one of your childhood fantasies, reality is usually pretty disappointing it turns out.

With Watson watching my back I lowered myself off the side of Colt's yacht and dropped down some six or seven feet to the ship docked down below. Landing in a low crouch I check the shadows to make sure I haven't been caught right off the rip. Somewhere above me the band changes tune. Something jaunty and upbeat. Not even the guards smoking cigarettes and talking amongst themselves seem to care.

Satisfied no one saw my little stunt, I make short work of crossing this boat and then it's onward and over to the next one. And the next one. And…well you get the idea. Brando's boat is last in line. The most northern docked yacht in this row. After that was only flat black water until the bay was interrupted by a thin stretch of peninsula known as Presque Isle State Park. Beyond that, more black water. And beyond that the Great White North.

I make it there without much of an issue. No gunfights. No karate. Just basically a casual stroll across some boats. It's literally a hop, skip, and jump away.

That said, I did say without much issue. I didn't say with no issue. It's the last jump that almost gets me. The distance was just a tad further than I had expected. I landed on Brando's yacht by the grip of my tippy toes. Heels dangling off the edge. Arms pin wheeling precariously. There's the terrible gut feeling that something is not as it should be. The inner ear protests in distortion. The cartoonish sense that should a calm breeze come along you'll be standing in mid-air with nothing more than a hand painted sign reading "Gulp!" before the plummet.

I tuck my chin to my chest and pitch myself forward. If there's one thing that I know well it's how to take a fall. Rule number 1: Don't panic. Rule number 2: Momentum is your friend. Rule number 3: Your body goes where your head goes. Four is basically embrace the moment, accept you're out of control, and do what you can to protect the parts of your body that would require an extended hospital visit to heal. Crunch yourself into a ball and basically ride the fall out.

Is my face plant onto the deck dignified? No. Is anything broken or otherwise severely wounded? Probably not. Am I in the drink? Negative Ghost Rider.

Maybe I'll just lay here for a minute. Make sure no one saw that. Take a few breaths to relax. In through the nose. Out through the mouth. There we go.

That's better.

I pick myself up into a low crouch with a grunt. I twist my shoulders until my spine snap crackle pops all the way down and take inventory of the situation. Point one: I've made it onto the boat. Point two: can confirm nothing is busted up. Doing good so far.

Brandon Lake might have not had old real estate money but he had had rockstar money. Just because his yacht was smaller didn't mean it was any less of a yacht. The type of boat you'd see on the water from the shore and say "Look a yacht." No one would correct you. Except maybe Scooby. He'd probably have something to say. He'd no doubt say something like "the tonnage is different. It has a shallower draft. You can tell by the subtle flaring of the bridge that this model of boat isn't a blah blah blah."

Or whatever he'd say.

To me it was a yacht if only a slightly shorter and squatter one than the one I'd started the evening on. Well, there's that and if we are comparing the two, I have to admit the one I left - as gaudy and gross as it was - was far better than the one I'm currently on. This one is gross for different reasons. If Colt's boat was the jewel of these waters, the great white pearl, then Brando's was the dingy and dark pirate ship lurking in the shadows off to the distance. Just waiting to pounce. Jet black hull. Modern sleek lines. Hell, it even had a tattered Jolly Roger hanging off the bow. It was everything Colt's gilded yacht was not.

The fact that it was also completely cracked out to the point of being a complete hot mess in the way that only a junky rockstar was capable of making it, really sold the difference home further.

I said early I wasn't ready to talk about my friend in a meaningful way, wellbeing on his boat - the last place anyone saw him alive and unwell - put me in a position that I sort of have to.

A man's environment is often a portrait of the man himself. And the man is often made up of a collection of circumstances leading him to where he is. Brando's collection of circumstances had led him down a road from abandoned youth to the band to the bottle to the pipe and finally to the needle. He'd found a surrogate family on the spoon with nothing about his last environment showing otherwise.

If you've never been to the junky's boneyard count yourself as lucky. It's not an experience you'll soon forget. Things aren't just messy, college dorms are just messy, no there's a deep, pervasive rot that seems to permeate everything and manifest everywhere as if the soul of the place itself has somehow been tainted.

The boneyard isn't just messy…it's madness.

Things are just off. Helter Skelter. It's one thing to have the assortment of parties past piled up, it is another thing entirely to have a collection of cum stained panties hanging from the deck lights like corpses hang from poles in dystopian nightmares. There's a propane grill wedged in the corner near an overturned wicker table. On it is a burnt pot of what I can only guess was at one point mac' n cheese.

Now you, me, our moms, we've all left a pot on the cooker overnight telling ourselves we will soak it tomorrow. That's pretty normal. Life gets busy. Things happen. No harm. Only someone deeply on the pipe would leave it there for weeks at a time. Whatever ecosystems have sprung up there are beyond human comprehension. There are more things in heaven and earth. Here there be monsters.

The abyss stares back.

The deck furniture is tangled in knotted Christmas lights despite it being the middle of summer. Then there are the electronics. Which are simply put:

Everywhere.

Everything is plugged into everything else in a confusing Rube Goldberg machine of potential electrical fires. Speakers wired into amps which are wired into subs then the whole rat's nest of wires snakes back into recorders and players.

A labyrinth of sound.

I pick myself up off the deck and take a step into the cabin. My heart nearly falls out of my ass when I am suddenly confronted by a life-sized plastic skeleton wearing a party hat and holding a half smoked Cuban between bony fingers. I take a deep breath to calm my nerves and immediately regret it.

It is the smell.

This place is a nightmare of scents.

Flop sweats mixed with a confusing assortment of candles and deodorizers. Rotting piles of grapefruit competes with stale beer and spilled gin. Aerosol deodorants advertising scents such as Alpine Peaks, Pure Sport, and Teen Spirit – whatever that is – jockey for position in my nose against decaying club sandwiches on a collection of silver serving trays. Every new smell seems to be designed to make me want to race to the railing and vomit my guts out into the harbor.

Worst of all is the junk stench.

Burnt chemicals and all kinds of wrong. This is the foul stench of the pipe and the needle. There's an almost physical reaction as the brain reacts in horror and tries to crawl out of your skull into some cave where it can be safe from this noxious assault.

This is all too much for one man.

"Took a few people down with you in your hot pipe didn't you Brando?" I ask no one in particular other than the skeleton. And what's he going to say? He's a fake Halloween skeleton.

Let's just get this done. Then we can be outta here. Before we go down with Brandon's ghost.

I make my way deeper into the cabin. I've been on this boat many times back before when it was still a boat and not a tomb or some kind of demented alter to forgotten eldritch horrors and bad decisions.

Been on it then too, but only for a brief moment before the madness became too much. You could say that I'm familiar.

I navigate through the dark by feel and by memory. The tingling 6th sense feeling that at every step a needle would appear protruding through my bare foot made the process slow going. Cautiously I moved from one semi clean spot to another. Hesitating every time I put my foot down. Like I said, it's a slow process.

Slower than I'd liked. I had no intention of spending more time here than I needed to. If I could have it my way I'd already be gone. Rushed in and then rushed off. However, to rush meant being treated for who knew what type of rare and horrifying diseases after having whatever it was that punctured the soft sole of my foot removed.

Fuck that.

We're taking it as slow as it goes.

If you've ever had the displeasure of having a junky friend you probably have gotten pretty good at what I like to call "Alice Thinking". It's a sort of acceptance of unreality, an understanding that what you are experiencing makes sense to someone, somewhere, just maybe not you. You have to tumble down the rabbit hole a bit if you are going to put yourself in the mind of a dope fiend.

If Brandon had any idea of what he'd created before he became too far gone, he'd probably come to the realization it would be worth something. That made it valuable. Unfortunately, valuable means something different to a junky. It's another way to score. Simple as that.

People on the pipe would sell their mothers if it meant staying on the pipe.

This fact should give me pause. I should at least consider that this tape isn't even here anymore and that it has been hawked off long ago for a gram or whatever the dealer has on hand. But I know Brandon Lake.

He'd sell his mother, sell his soul, sell his flash cars and expensive watches, but he'd pitch proper hell about selling his music. It was something his label hated about him. Lake Effect in Affect's first two albums were an unmitigated nightmare to release with Brando fighting every contract every step of the way. His music wasn't made for that.

If anything, it was made to exist in rebellion to everything the record labels stood for. Capitalism. Consumerism.

So, no. He wouldn't have hawked it.

Which meant he would have kept it safe.

And where do you keep things safe? In a safe. Obviously.

AR Bennett

Which just so happens to be exactly where I remembered one being. On the back wall in the master bedroom, behind a picture of John and Robert Kennedy shaking hands. Someone has painted bloody red slashes over the brother's eyes.

Dead Kennedys indeed.

I pull down the portrait and peer at the safe. My eyes have gotten adjusted to the gloom of the yacht's interior, and the full moon helps by sending some light my way through a porthole. It's a pretty standard affair as far as safes go. Steel face. Metal hinges. Lever.

Combination lock.

Oops.

That could be a bit of an issue.

Despite being from the other side of the tracks I'm not the type of bad to be a professional safecracker. I didn't have a drill or crowbar tucked up somewhere in my slacks. No stethoscope stashed up in the old prison wallet either. This combination could be any number of things. Three-digit code. Ten digits counting 0 each. Thousands of possibilities. Millions maybe? Math is hard. Point is someone could spend all night and into next week just turning this dial hoping to get lucky.

And okay. I get it. I can hear you saying "You came all this way and you don't have a plan to open the safe"? Yeah. Yeah. Loud and clear.

"Right. That's going to be an issue."

Think like how a junky would have…thank? Thunk? I look around the safe a bit hoping for a post-it-note with a helpful code written on it that realistically should have been nearby. Unfortunately, Lady Luck isn't taking my calls at the moment. Okay. Okay.

Okay.

I retrace my steps and make my way into the other rooms before finally climbing a ladder up into the helm. Everything is just as horrible up here as it had been down in the bowels of the ship - boat. Yacht. Whatever - after a cursory examination I come up with nothing. Now I've got a few options running through my head. I'm fairly certain Scooby has the technical know-how or at the very least the patience to get this safe opened. And if that fails Alaska could just beat it open with his bare hands.

If I'm going to do that route, I'd need to get both of them here to the boat. Unless…

Unless I were to bring the boat to them! Now that's a

Thought.

That's the word.

Think like a junky would have thought. Duh. Way to prove your English teachers right Saint. Here I am a grown ass man taking a tense conjugation test and still getting big fat zeroes.

"Oh…" I can't help but laugh out loud to myself. "Would it really be that easy? Really?"

Worth a shot, I guess.

This is Brandon Lake we're talking about. I make my way back down to the master bedroom and once again slide the portrait over only this time instead of standing there all confuzzled I reach for the combination lock and spin the dial.

Zero right.

Zero left.

Zero right.

The lock clicks open with a satisfying clank leaving me to gawk at it with a dumbfounded amusement that is both grateful and deeply saddened by how far down the rabbit hole my friend had gone. If I needed more proof Brandon Lake was a junky this would be it.

Junkies by their nature wouldn't think it at all odd to keep their prized positions safe in a - well - safe only to set the combination for the thing to its default. Wouldn't even cross their minds. Nothing about that would seem strange to your average junk user. That's just standard operating procedure.

I pull the handle down and the safe comes open. It's full of stuff. That's the best way I can come up with to describe it. Not sure what I was expecting, if I was expecting anything at all, but there was actually a bit of this and that in here. A pack of condoms. A dirty leopard print thong. A bag of Columbian Bam Bam. A few joints. You know. The important things. There was a signed headshot of Brandon signed by himself.

To himself.

Chips from Caesars Palace. A check for $30,000 from a record label left uncashed. All things considered, there was actually quite a lot in the safe.

What wasn't in the safe, as far as I could tell, was one genre altering punk rock album worth one and a half million dollars. Instead under all the clutter there's just a thick manilla folder bound in rubber bands. I pull it out and skim the contents in the dark half-light. Official. Governmental. Bar graphs and line charts. Blueprints. It all looks Greek to me. All very complicated and confusing schematics to…something.

I don't know a lot about albums other than how to listen to them, but what I do know is that they usually aren't whatever this is.

If the tape isn't here,

Then where is it?

I'm about to start over at square one and give the place a more thorough searching when something outside the boat catches my attention. A new noise that wasn't there before. It's hard to make out but it sounds a bit like concerned voices yelling. Under and through that there is the sound of a large engine revving up and water being pushed aside.

    I fold up the file and jam it as securely as I can into my suit coat. It's a tight fit, what with the thickness of the file and all, but I make it work. Just wedge it in there if you will. I also grab the blow because why not I guess?

    Keeping low I start to make my way away from the safe with the hopes of taking a bit more time to toss the place even if that felt impossible with its current tossed state.

    A blaring boat horn stops me dead in my tracks. I turn to look to the starboard - which is right for all you land lubbers out there - and my corneas are nearly seared out of the back of my head from a brilliant and blinding light.

    Then things get a bit weird.

AR Bennett

Track Seven: Penis Envy

Now I can tell you what happened after it happened, or I can show you what happened while it is happening.

I can't do both.

This median we find ourselves in is a great many things, but visual is not one of them. Which is a shame because what happened deserves to be seen. It is, after all, very cinematic. Not in the way my little speech was cinematic mind. This isn't the golden age so much as it is Roland Emmerich. The new generation. Spielberg, Scott, Cameron, Woo, and Bay. Style over substance. Big set pieces over plot. What Ebert might call

"A popcorn flick"

As in: A motion picture without serious dramatic content, a weighty message, or intellectual depth, which serves simply as enjoyable entertainment. Pulp. Brain candy. An action movie.

In this moment of absurdity, as with most moments of high-octane stress, time slows. Hummingbird heartbeats become the long deep rumble of tectonic plates shifting under the deep ocean. Panting breaths are measured in minutes not seconds. As adrenaline spikes the normal rules of the world spin off their axis. You are no longer in control. The natural drug, your body's primordial defense mechanism, has taken the reins leaving you a hapless bystander in the events.

Fight.

Flight.

Or freeze.

This outer body experience is all a very sciencey way of saying: from the moment the boat horn blasted through the drugged out and decaying yacht…

The normal rules no longer applied

*****

AR Bennett

FADE IN

BARNABY J. COLT - late 50s with gray perfectly barbered hair wearing a very expensive tuxedo, watch, and leather shoes - stands at the helm of his yacht. He gestures wildly spilling amber scotch from a crystal glass as he talks. Behind him equally gray men in equally fancy, through cheaper, tuxedos nod in agreement.

                    COLT

This bad boy has over 2,500 horsepower. Top of the line diesel engines made custom from Hamburg. You'd think a beast this big wouldn't be responsive, but I'll tell you what gentlemen...she can put my Porsche through its paces.

The gathered hanger ons nod and feign interest as they sip their own scotches and puff at Cuban cigars. Behind them the captain in a crisp white uniform looks on with growing unease. His sea hardened face is etched with worry lines. And why shouldn't it be? Colt - who isn't a trained ship captain but is however his sole employer- is awfully close to the throttle lever.

                    COLT

They wanted $300,000 for these engines and you know what I did? Do you? I paid them for it. Those greedy immigrants. You can't put a price on power now can you gents? Course not! Of course not.

Colt's hand is now resting on the throttle. The captain takes a tentative step forward but shrinks back behind the trust fund brigade after a white-hot stare comes his way from his boss.

                    COLT
            Want a demonstration?

There are a few skeptical nods. These elder statesmen have had enough scotch that just about anything could be a good idea, but they look at the captain expecting him to step up. He does not.

                    COLT
    That is the point of owning a yacht is it not? To feel the wind at your back and the spray on your face. Let's take her out.

He presses the throttle lever forward slightly. A distant rumble from the bowels of the ship reverberates up through the mahogany deck.

                THE CAPTAIN
                    Sir?

                    COLT
    Step back. This is my ship. Mine. I'll be damned if I can't take her out.

Colt's hand on the throttle pushes up a notch and the vibrations grow in intensity. The big ship lurches forward. Colt smiles and his guests feel obliged to smile back.

                THE CAPTAIN
                  Uh…Aye sir.

   He spins on his heel in a frantic unsure motion. and calls to the crew.

AR Bennett

                    THE CAPTAIN
            Raise anchor! The anchor damnit! Now!

The other guests below deck in the ballroom and staterooms can now feel the movement. Crystal glasses shake on deck tables and wicker chairs move about.

WATSON - late 20s / early 30s dressed as described previously - looks down at her glass as it skitters about with concern.

                       WATSON
            Oh shit…shit shit shit…Saint.

As the crew hurriedly try and get the anchors up the boat moves forward. This yacht - bigger than all the rest in the yacht club's docks - begins to pull out of its slip.

CUT TO

A smaller, more modern, yacht at the end of the docks. Its black hull is nearly invisible against the dark waters of the bay behind. Inside there is SAINT -roguishly handsome, hero type, with a devil-may-care looks and attitude to match - he's stuffing a file into the breast pocket of his suit coat. There's a sense he is in a place he shouldn't be.

An echoing ship horn cuts through the night. It's loud enough to startle our hero and he rushes to a nearby porthole with a jump.

                        SAINT
                 What the fuuuu….

Blinding light from the bigger ship's bow streams through the porthole and assaults Saint's face. He lifts up a hand to shield his eyes, blinking rapidly to get his sense of sight back. From Saint's perspective the bigger yacht towers above him and is looming ever closer. The boat horn blasts again.

SAINT
What the hell is that crazy old bastard doing?

Colt's yacht lurches closer. Rooster tails of spray shoot up from the stern of the ship as big brass screws begin to turn faster. There's that classic fast cut montage scene showing each part of an engine roaring to life. Pistons pumping. Cranks turning. Fuel igniting.

SAINT
Abandon ship!

Saint spins around from the porthole and begins a mad scramble to try and get out of the ship. He trips over the furniture and crashes through the dark until he makes his way up onto the deck. Behind him Colt's boat takes up the entire horizon and hangs over Saint's position in the way we think of gods as enormous.

Thinking on pure instinct Saint darts to the starboard side facing open water. He's just about to make a dive off the side when the two ships collide in an ear-splitting scream of twisted metal. The impact is so intense Saint is flung from the deck and lands a solid 10 yards away with a splash.

Then it's
   CUT TO BLACK

Track Eight: Germfree Adolescence

In my line of work I do my level best to avoid speaking to the cops in any meaningful fashion. This is an almost required trait. Nothing good ever comes from talking to the cops. To achieve this, I do my level best to avoid cops entirely. I've gotten a fairly good streak going.

Which makes this evening all the sadder that I'm now forced to talk to these two.

"So, what were you doing on the other boat then Mr....?" The taller of the cops asks. Pen posed over little notepad ready to jot down all the details. Just the facts ma'am. He seems to be the diligent one.

"Smith. John Smith. Smitty to my friends."

"So, what were you doing on the other boat then Mr. Smith?"

That's a good question. What was I doing on that other boat? Clearly not finding what I had come for that's what. They don't need to know that though.

"I wasn't."

"You weren't?" This is from the second shorter cop. The one without the pen and pad and eager beaver attitude. The one not too old for this shit just yet but that's only because he's a loose cannon who doesn't play by the rules but still somehow gets results.

"I was not."

"If that's the case then why did my partner and I have to fish you out of the drink on the other boat." The tall one asks. I can feel the pair doing this back and forth in a practiced way of setting the snare and ping ponging back and forth until the trap is tripped.

The last thing I want to be doing right now is being questioned by two plain clothe donut munchers. I'm soaking wet and slightly shivering in the back of an ambulance. Someone has draped a silver thermal blanket over my shoulders.

You've seen this scene before.

The red and blue gum drops of police lights casting flickering shadows as first responders respond to the calamity in the background. In this case two yachts tangled together like violent lovers and slowly listing deeper into the lake. Off to my right, standing arms crossed and in serious discussion, Watson speaks with someone who has all the hallmarks of a seasoned, grizzled, detective. The ten-dollar haircut. Bad suit. Worn leather shoes with a demeanor just as weathered. Watson is clearly agitated. Throwing her hands about, face flush with hot anger. I wonder what she is saying? And how deep into her bag of tricks she is digging?

"Can you explain it further for us Mr. Smith?" The short cop pulls my attention back to the interrogation. He looks at me impatiently with a certain persistence that permeates into how the pen in his hand taps on the little spiral bound notebook. Tap tap tap.

Sure. I had snuck onto a private party by manipulating my friend's connections to secure a plus one. Then I went over the side and hopped over several other pieces of private property in order to reach my dead rockstar friend's ship where I aimed to pillage and pilfer my black heart out for profit and glory. Should I walk to the gallows myself or would you prefer to take me?

Not tonight.

AR Bennett

I thought and I thunk until my thinker was sore. I needed to come up with something and come up with it quick. Lickety split. Luckily, I'm a sneaky fox. Luckier still I am what some might consider a bit obsessed with the cinema. A cinephile if you will.

"Titanic."

Maybe I should have thunk on that some more. Both of the cops seemed to think so. They looked at me like I had tentacles growing out of my ears. They looked at each other the way partners do and shrugged the way partners shrugged. Simultaneously.

"Titanic? Leo and Kate? Jack and Rose? Come on guys it was a pretty big deal. James Cameron actually went down there ya know? In like a sub."

"Are you saying that the reason we found you where you were was because you were on the other boat doing king of the world from Titanic?" The short cops says through a growing cloud of confusion. His partner gives him that "How would you know" look and he shrugs. "I…err…My wife loves that film. But is that what you're saying?"

"No."

"No?"

"No. What I am saying is I was on this ship doing king of the world from Titanic when I was thrown from this ship to that ship. Does that track?"

"Yes." / "No." Now the pair is confused with each other. On one hand you have someone who seems to know a great deal about a summer romance film which feels counter to cop's usual need to watch nothing more than macho mega action flicks. On the other you have the diligent one being diligent and trying to jot down just what in the hell this soaking wet fast talking potential perp is jimmer jammering on about.

I put my head in my hands and let out a frustrated sigh. This wasn't my best work. Not even close. But it's popped into my possibly concussed head at a time when any thought would do. Things had certainly gone off the rails around here. And I was hoping that would be enough to sell this bill of goods.

Why not? A party guest on the bow of the ship, taking in the scotch and the night air, gets compelled to do the whole king of the world pose only to be far flung clear onto another boat when the two collide.

The more you say it the more it makes sense.

But the cops are still arguing among themselves, and this is a place I'd rather not be. I pinch the bridge of my nose and shake water out of my ears.

"So, you're saying that you're a guest of Mr. Colt's then Mr. Smith?" Finally, the tall one manages to wrangle his partner back on track.

"No."

"No?"

"No. What I'm saying is that I was a guest of one of Mr. Colt's guests. A plus one."

The short cops seems to look incredulous. He has the air of the type of person who opens their mouth and whatever train of thought chugging along in there just tumbles out. "I thought women could only be plus ones?"

"Jesus Christ." Me and the tall cop say simultaneously. At least we're getting on the same page. That's got to be progress, right?

Only it isn't. It's the opposite in fact. The two cops begin this awkward tango of back and forth leaving my head twitching left and right like I'm at a tennis match. I try to interject but I am met with a raised finger from the tall one telling me to hold my horses. So, I do. Saddle them up tight and just sit there in the back of the meat wagon tapping my toes to a beat only I can hear. I'm not really a patient person.

I know patience is a virtue.

But I'm not that kind of saint.

Finally, after what feels like forever the short cop turns back to me and resumes his line of questioning. "Are you aware the boat we found you on is a potential crime scene?"

"Yes."

"You are aware that boat is a potential crime scene? How would you know that?"

"Well, some idiot just crashed his mega yacht into the side of it. I can personally attest that said idiot was also a drunk idiot. That's got to be DUI – well BUI I guess – at the bare minimum. Boating Under the Influence is still a crime, correct?"

"That's a different matter." The tall cop states. "Altogether."

Me and the short cop shrug and look directly at him. Together in unison we respond with "That's a different matter."

Nailed it.

What happens next isn't worth noting. It goes on like this for quite some time. We can just speed things up a touch and I'll bring you back in when we get to the important parts.

Around me the world seems to pick up tempo. Cops move about in a blur of motion. Other guests being questioned speed run through their testimonies. The waves on the lake come fast and steady as time moves at 2.5x speeds. Black cars arrive. Guests in tuxes depart. Some cops go here. Others there. All the while the two tasked with dealing with me continue their back and forth only now it's too fast to hear the words. What would have taken several hours is condensed down into moments.

"So, am I free to go?"

"Yes. For now. We'll be in touch. Get yourself checked out at the hospital and don't leave town."

I had no intentions of doing either. As the cops walked back to their cruiser, I gathered my still wet suit coat from under my legs where I'd been discreetly sitting on it and shrugged out of the thermal blanket. The club was basically deserted now. Even Watson was nowhere to be found. Which wasn't entirely unexpected. This isn't the Navy and we're not the SEALS. If you fall behind you get left behind to find your own way out. Those are the rules.

Plus, Watson is connected.

What would her family think?

Tucking my jacket – and the folder hidden within – under my arm I walk away from the ambulance and away from the front gate. I'm already wet so I don't mind wading in the shallows around the club's fence. The sand feels soft under my feet. My shoes have obviously gone down with the ship.

With a resigned sigh I start the not so insignificant walk down the beach back to my neck of the woods. The thin beach is a mix of sand and rock and stretches out in both directions. To the east is the lights of downtown with the brightest being the Bicentennial Tower that overlooks the bay. To the west is Kelso Beach and my Kelso Beach House.

Familiar ground and home turf.

There is hardly any light this way save for a few homes perched up on the cliff face overlooking the water. Luckily the midnight moon is fat and full in the cloudless sky so navigating my way back isn't all that much of a challenge. Not like I needed it.

AR Bennett

I have this strip of sand mostly memorized. I'm from here. Grew up here. This is my stomping grounds. I could probably get my way back blindfolded and by feel and memory alone. Soon the soft sound of waves replaces the sounds of sirens and I put one foot in front of the other almost on autopilot.

By the time I was halfway back my suit had started to dry in that uncomfortable stiff chafing way. We weren't meant to wear suits. You can't swim in a suit. Unless it is of the swimsuit variety. I was head down and trying not to rip off my slacks and chuck them into the lake when two large menacing shadows materialized in front of me well…for lack of a better word…menacingly.

They stepped out of the dark and I could immediately tell where my night was probably heading. Big guys. Shaved heads like ogres and hands like shovels. Brightly colored Hawaiian shirts barely concealing bulging muscles full of hardly restrained malice and HGH.

Then there's these two.

Fuck.

Whose cosmic Cheerios had I pissed in?

"Nice night for a romantic stroll huh boys? Welp. I'll leave you to it then."

A meaty hand covered in tattoos and scars stops me. I smile the smile of a man who really shouldn't be smiling but that's just sort of a reaction I've built up over years of these sort of interactions.

"I'm honored. Flattered really. But uh you aren't my type. No offense."

It's hard to tell these two apart. They are both of similar shape, size, and overall Russianness. The dumb looking one, and they are both dumb looking, steps behind me and blocks off that potential exit.

The first one smiles a humorless smile, gold tooth catching the moonlight.

"Miss Mikhailov would like her property." He says in a voice made of sandpaper and rockslides. "Now."

"I didn't catch your name."

"Ivan."

"What about him?" I gesture behind me with my chin.

"Ivan."

"You're both Ivan? That makes it easy to remember, I guess. You know I once had two cousins named Jim. Brothers. Jim and Jim. Neither wanted to go by James or Jake or The Blonde One. Super confusing. Especially at family…"

The first hit comes from behind and puts my kidneys in contact with other parts of my body that it shouldn't be chummy with. Air goes out of my lungs and I grit my teeth together against the pain.

"The Tape." The dumb one, the one who sucker punched me, threatens. His voice is actually almost cartoonishly high pitched which comes as a surprise coming from a man of his stature.

"I don't have it."

"It wasn't in safe?" He squeaks in his sucking helium way.

Well, that's interesting. Here I was thinking I'd have a sure thing being one of the only people still sober enough to know about the safe. Then it clicks.

SMASH CUT TO:

The Ivans board Brando's yacht and begin to do their thug thing. They rummage through this or that and turn over that or this. They search in drawers and closets and under the couch leaving no spot untouched by their rubber gloved fingers.

When they get to the portrait of the Kennedy brothers, they pull it off the wall and boom there's the safe. The dumb one reaches for the dial and turns it a few times. Pulls the handle. Nothing.

They shrug in the way partners do.

Walking off the boat they duck under yellow police caution tape and walk up to two plain clothes cops standing guard. A tall one and a short one. You know the type. Gold tooth Ivan slides a thick envelope out of from his pocket and discreetly presses it into the short cop's hands. The pair of partners nod and the Ivan's go about their way.

*****

"Rubber gloves. Smart. That place was disgusting and I thought it felt tossed, well more tossed than usual."

"Da. The tape."

"Listening to all that communist bullshit can't be good for someone's ears. Maybe you didn't hear me but I don't have it. If Ali…" The next set of punches is a one two combo on each of my sides. "…ugh. If Miss Mikhailov wants a status report, she can come to the bar herself and we'll talk."

"You opened the safe da?"

"I don't know if you know this but the whole thing went tits up when some fucking rich prick took us down in a goddamn broadside." This time there's no hits from behind. But there is one from the font.

Gold Tooth Ivan hits me so hard I have time to see Tweety Birds and stars before I hear the sickening sound of my nose cracking. Crimson globs come out of both nostrils and go flinging off into the night. My knees buckle and I fall forward only to be bounced off of Gold Tooth Ivan into Dumb Looking Ivan who pushes me forward again this time down onto the sand.

Where I stay.

To them it looks like I am groaning and moaning. Frantically trying to hold my nose together but in actuality…

Well, I'm groaning and moaning and trying to hold my fucking nose together. I keep one hand on my shattered beak and try to unsuccessfully massage the cartilage back into place. With my other hand though…

…with my other hand I'm actually doing something clever.

This isn't my first broken nose after all. And my hands can be rather sleight when I need them to be. Say what you will about us riff raff most of it is just harmful stereotypes and I pay it no mind. But the fast hands and sticky fingers bit? Let's just say sometimes you gotta know how to make a living.

Dumb Ivan yanks me up and holds me steady while Gold Tooth Ivan begins to search my pockets. It's a proper pat down. TSA would approve. When he finds nothing, he nods and his partner lets go of me where I again fall to the sand in a heap. Bloody and beaten.

Just where I want them.

"Look. The job is still on. It wasn't where I thought it would be, but that doesn't mean I can't still get it right?"

I look up with all the pleading puppy dog eyes and milk the pity card for all it's worth. Don't hurt me boys. I'm only little. "I just need some more time and Al…" I watch as Ivan raises his fist and quickly course correct. "Miss Mikhailov will have what she paid for."

AR Bennett

The Ivans confer amongst themselves with unspoken grunts and nods. Very cavemen like this lot.

"Twenty-four hours. Da?"

From down in the sand, I give a mock salute and sling blood all over Gold Tooth Ivan's shoes. He grunts in disapproval and kicks sand at my face forcing me to speak through a mouth of grit. "Da comrade."

Dumb Ivan gives one last kick into my ribs before the pair continue off down the beach. I'm curled up in a ball all thank yous and see ya soons and appreciations of them taking it easy on me. Right up until they are around a bend and out of sight.

Then I drop the act, pick myself up from the sand, and pull out the folder where I had buried it after the first – second? – punch.

Well now there's that.

I haven't been fully honest with you. It's not lying if it is omitting some of the truth, right? Turns out the whole tape thing wasn't entirely just my idea. I had a bit of help. Some direction if you will. Deals made. Hands shook. That sort of thing.

Now I just had to keep my end of the bargain.

Brushing myself off I chewed on the wet sand that clogged my mouth thoughtfully. Twenty-four hours and I had already taken my best shot. There would be no more helpful ideas or directions. It was finding this tape or it would be

"Do svidaniya Comrade Saint." I spit out the bloody sand and wipe my mouth with my suit sleeve. Why not? It's ruined anyway. Nothing a bit of blood would do at this point.

Here's hoping Bones and Alaska had better luck tonight.

I tucked the folder safely back into my jacket and put feet to sand with a quickness. Almost as if I didn't have time to waste.

Because I didn't.

AR Bennett

Track Nine: Nevermind

It was what most people would consider late by the time I got back to the Kelso Beach House. To the Bad Bunch however this was considered still pre-game time. The party didn't get started in earnest around here until well *well* after the sun went down. 1AM was just the before party. Then there was the party. Then the post party wrap up. Then the boozy brunch.

The Bunch minus Watson was right where I left them when I stumbled in. Scooby, Alaska, Benny Bones, Rob's Sister, and Handsome Black sat around the card table and were deep in a game of what best can be described as illegal five card poker meets binge drinking. Equal parts card hustle and blackout. The best type of game if you ask me.

Rob's Sister was first to see me come in and she gave off this little "Well hello there" smile. We have history. It's a whole thing. Then she sees the blood soaking down my shirt turning it from starch white to a wet pink and that smile turns into more of a concerned although not entirely unexpected frown.

"There he is!" Benny Bones says as I come around. "Whoa. Sheesh. Patron Saint of The Broken and Beaten huh? Rough night bro? You look like hell."

"Shouldn't you be at the boneyard?" I snap. Bones gives me this indignant look. Alaska and him share a glance before both simultaneously shrugging.

Which tells me all I need to fucking know. Still though, I shouldn't have shown teeth and bit Bones's head off like that. It's not like it is his fault. "Sorry Benny. It's been a night. Scoob? Might I have a word with you in the office?"

Scooby doesn't look up from his cards. "No."

Oh, so he's still riding the I told you so train, is he? Well fine. If that's how he wants to play it.

I begin to slide my wet slacks off and give him the full moon. The Bunch laughs it up. A few drunk ladies at the bar whistle. Scooby looks up and shakes his head. He's got a mortified expression chiseled into his features.

"I'll make it worth your while."

"Jesus there's customers Saint." He slides out of his chair and apologizes to the four or five ladies at the bar. What do they care? Free show.

Plus, this isn't a real bar.

I snag two beers from the card table and march off. Pants still half off I walk into the back office where I fully undress and yank on a pair of boardshorts and a t-shirt. Scooby comes in a moment later and closes the door behind him.

"I take it things did not go well then?"

"You could say that yeah."

"Is all that from the crash?" He asks referring to my face.

"How do you know about that?" I ask after slamming the top off a beer on the desk cutting a deep gouge into the wood. Scooby bristles at my constant disregard for our furniture but wisely chooses to say nothing about it.

"Come on. It's a small town, Saint. An incident like that is better than reality tv."

"What the fuck is reality tv?" The first beer goes down so fast I barely notice that I've already popped the top and am onto the second.

"Like…Real Housewives?" Scooby stammers and immediately regrets he has.

"You watch something called 'Real Housewives'?"

He shakes his head and waves his hand in the air as if to clear away this conversation. "What happened to your face?"

"You know that posh princess that came in a few nights back? The ice maiden?"

Scooby nods his head. It's not like him or anyone other hotblooded male and some hotblooded female members of the Bad Bunch would soon forget.

"She's Alisa Mikhailov."

I need to step back a bit to allow Scooby to spit his beer out and have it not land on my clean(ish) shirt. When he is done choking, he sets the bottle down on the desk and fixes me with one of those "What the hell man" Scooby looks.

"Alisa Mikhailov as in Boris Mikhailov's daughter?" He asks.

"Correct."

"As in Boris Mikhailov as in Boris the Bloody Butcher Mikhailov? His daughter? His only daughter?"

"Correct again."

"Didn't he?"

"He did"

"Jesus," Scooby says clearly taken a bit aback. "With a pencil?"

"A ballpoint pen actually."

Let me tell you a story. Once upon a time in Moscow the penniless child of a gulag Boris Mikhailov decides he isn't happy with the card's he's been dealt in life and decides to change the game. Make it his game. His rules. Stacks the deck so that only he can win. It's a long and bloody couple of decades for young Boris but pretty soon he is penniless no more. In fact, he is one of the top-ranking head honchos of a Stazi backed crime organization that spans from Moscow to South Asia to Londongrad.

Communism hasn't slowed these boys down. Not one bit.

Boris and his crew? They run all the dark ponies in that neck of the woods. Drugs. Guns. Racketeering. Loan Sharking. Murder for hire. Prostitution. You name it as a vice and Boris the Butcher has his fingers in that pie.

Only Russia is changing. Maybe not all that better but changing nonetheless. They like being invited to the Olympics. Want to be thought of as a real and true nation, more than that a real and true superpower. And real and true superpowers don't let gangsters infiltrate everything up to and including high government.

Unless you're the US of A of course. But that's a story for Tom Clancy to tell.

So, the new USSR has started putting the screw into Boris and his brand of bad. Crack downs. Investigations. And a brave intrepid reporter gets a nose for a scope. The smell of hot ink. Story of the century. Which Boris the Butcher can't have. He's Boris the Butcher not Boris the Bud. So, he finds out where this would be Woodward is hiding out and then kills him, his family, and his dog with a ballpoint pen. Or maybe it was several ballpoint pens.

Who can say.

Not that it matters if it was one or several because a true bad underworld legend is born. Now The Butcher is too hot to handle. Has his own satellite. Wiretaps. Informants. Red Notice. The whole kit and kaboodle. He packs up his dirty bloody bags of rubles and makes a break for the wild wild West. Why he decided to lay low and rebuild in Erie Fucking Pennsylvania of all places no one really knows.

AR Bennett

Maybe the brutal winters here remind him of home.

Whatever the reason Boris the Butcher has set up shop on our shores and has since started buying or bullying his way into all the dark ponies around here. Up to his old tricks and back at it again as it were.

And now there's me and his daughter.

Oops.

"This is the part where you tell me it was all innocent right?" Scooby asks after the shock has worn off a bit.

"It was innocent. We just had drinks."

"Just drinks huh?"

Red lipsticks on white cigarettes. Her giving me the eyes. Me giving her the eyes. Head nods and backrooms. Her dress coming unzipped. My boardshorts coming untied. Then it's all fast cuts and sudden edits.

Her on top.

Me on top.

Hands gripping hips.

Legs over shoulders.

Moaning.

Groaning.

Bam bam bam. One after another in quick rapid-fire succession until the whole scene blurs together in a scrapbook sort of collage of heated images and scandalous memories. When it finally slows down to linger on one scene for long enough the two of us are in tangled sheets, smoking, staring at the ceiling fan slowly spinning. She looks over at me and says, "I've got a job for you."

"Yep. Just drinks."

"So here I am to assume that you're bringing this up because she's involved in this whole tape thing then?" Scooby is pretty perceptive when he wants to be. He's already pieced it together no doubt and is just wanting and waiting for me to confirm it.

"Something like that."

"How involved?"

Red nails piercing skin on my back. Toes curling. Auburn hair flowing wild in the fake wind of the fan.

"Fairly. She's the buyer."

"Doesn't strike me as a fan of hardcore punk."

Me either. But who am I to judge? We all have our things. She said she fell in love with the sound. The rage of it. Had to get her hands on the last album of the late great bad boy from the Mistake on The Lake. Willing to pay top for it too. Which as you know, and everyone else around here seems to constantly forget, we could really use the cash at the moment.

"No one pays a yard for an album Saint. Lost or otherwise."

He's not going to like this part. I can tell already by his mood.

"She's involved with him." I mumble around my beer. Scooby's face goes whiter than usual and he has the look of a man who'd very much like to punch something. Which he just might when he hears the rest. "With Brandon. They have history."

When Scooby finally unclenches his jaw, his tone is low and full of accusations. "And now the two of you have history."

"We have a business agreement if that's what you mean."

"I'm going to go out on a limb here and say the nose wasn't from the crash then?" He asks and I shake my head. Faster than I'd like because for a brief moment I count stars circling the dingy ceiling tiles.

"Couple of heavies. Two Ivans."

"Wanting the tape which you don't have?"

"No Scoob, they saw me coming down the beach and hated my nose. Hated how I breathed out of it. Yes, they wanted the fucking tape and no I obviously don't have it or else it would be bottle service up in here instead of bloody fucking bandages."

I'm snapping again. Not his fault. But sometimes you just have to direct your rage at something or someone. My head hurts too much for stupid questions and potential lectures. I finish the beer and fetch the bottle of bourbon I keep hidden in the desk. That should help.

"None of this seemed odd to you? The daughter of a mass murderer mafioso coming down from the high ivory heavens and having a drink before giving an offer to good to refuse. That wasn't a bit off?"

Well, when you put it like that. But to be fair I was a bit distracted. Can you blame a guy? Still, this wasn't entirely solely on me either. I am just doing what needs to be done to keep the lights on around here. There's a higher purpose happening here. Nobility. Generosity. Helping others help themselves. Those that can should.

Or whatever.

It's not like that lot was out there finding ways to make yards. No that had to fall on me. As always.

"So, if this tape wasn't on the boat then where is it?"

"Not sure. Bones and Alaska came up empty too. And before you start cut em some slack, I pulled them from the Canadian thing. My orders." I pull out the thick sandy and still damp folder from my jacket and lay it out on the table. Scooby leans in to have a look. "But I did find this."

While Scooby studies the folder's contents, I test which one of my nostrils still has some semblance of sucking power. The little baggy of giddy up I pilfered from Brando's safe along with the folder seems to be exactly what the doctor ordered. My brain needs a pick-me-up. Something to jumpstart the synapses and knock away the cobwebs.

The problem is, no matter how I angle my nose, or which nostril I pinch shut, or tweak this or that it just ain't doing. The nose beers stay stubbornly in the little bag and I'm left still foggy and groggy and a few steps behind.

Frustrated I put the powder into a drawer in the desk and study the file over Scoob's shoulder. Still just Greek. Still just squiggly lines on soggy pages.

Scooby's finished with the files. He too shrugs. Seems stumped as much as I am.

"This feels more Colt Industries than Stalingrad. Do you think he's involved somehow?"

"When isn't he involved somehow?"

I don't know for certain though. Wheels spinning. Thoughts racing. I'm not certain of anything at the moment. But I do know one thing.

"Right. Whatever is going on under the surface is secondary. First things first. We gotta find that tape. Here's what you're going to do. Round up Alaska, Bones, Handsome Black and whatever other heavies you can scrape together. Get some bar flies off stools if you have to. But you go out and you hit the streets and you hit them hard. Brando was never a shy guy. Whatever he was into he would be rambling on about it to anyone dumb enough or smacked out enough to listen. Flip some flop houses. Turn the lights on and catch the scattering roaches. No stone unturned got it?"

AR Bennett

Someone knows something. They have to. Scooby folds up the folder and slips it away. I don't have to ask him to keep it safe. He knows. We're partners after all. He looks at me curiously, concern starting to creep in around the corners of his dark eyes.

He shouldn't worry. I'm fine.

This is fine.

Just mobilize the troops and put on the pressure.

"Scoob, hit it hard. But if someone isn't talkative you punch them or you pay them. We're not the mafia."

"No, you just seem to have fallen in bed with them."

Too true. Too late to do anything about it now though. Wheels were in motion and the streets had already started to come alive with the sounds of violence and pain.

Scooby and I walk out of the back office and are immediately jumped by Handsome Black.

Speak of the devil. His ears must have been burning.

We call Handsome Black 'Handsome Black' because he is handsome and it just so happens that he is black. Now this might seem halfhearted on our part, but it is more his doing than ours. Handsome has this habit of answering any inquiry directed at him with - And I quote:

"Yes, because I'm black."

Say it enough and the name sort of sticks, remember?

We added the handsome bit because the flash fucker is a goddamn GQ model. Or could have been had he been born in NYC or LA and not this sinking town on the lake. By and large Handsome Black is the best looking out of the Bunch, and that's with me on the list. I'd like to envision I set a fairly high bar but that could just be me being me.

"Saint. Scooby." Handsome nods by way of greeting. "Might I have a word with the both of you?"

"We just finished up having words HB." I say hurriedly. Handsome Black is not just handsome (or black) he can also chat your damn ear off if you give him a minute. Great story teller. Funny as hell. Not the time. "Now's not the best bro."

"It's about the Canadians."

Shit.

Them.

This day just won't quit now will it?

I subconsciously rub the faded scar cut through my left eyebrow and go to pinch my nose in thought, remember my nose is broken to shit and withdraw my fingers with a wince and grimace, before turning to Scooby for assistance.

"What about them?" He asks for me.

Handsome shrugs and puts his hands up in that "Don't shoot the messenger" motion. "They want a word."

I groan and shake my head furiously trying to get some sense of back to the basics in there. Jesus The H Stands For Holy Shit Christ. I don't need this right now. Don't I have people for this sort of thing? Doesn't anyone work around here?

"What about?" Scooby asks. He waves his bony hands to hurry up our flash friend and keep him from rambling. I'm still shaking my head like a wet dog and making strange guttural sounds that oscillate between annoyance and pain.

Scooby and I are doing the nonverbal communication that can only be understood between us because we have been in the same trenches, side by side, for so long. Even still, I am getting the feeling whatever I am trying to convey isn't exactly coming through crystal clear like. Scooby is switching between Handsome and me as his eyebrow creeps up higher under his scruffy hair.

"You know them." Handsome says with another shrug from a well sculpted and caramel shoulder. "Shipments are behind and they are concerned. Not too concerned - not like they were rude about asking for the chat - Canadians being Canadians." Scooby waves his hands in increasingly faster circles. Handsome nods. "Just want a meet that's all. Make sure we're all good."

Scooby strokes his beard in much the same way that I rub my scars. Habitual. Lost in thought. A thinker's thinking gesture. He looks at me and I just shrug. Head gripped in my hands. You take point on this one Scoob. Not like you're not invested as much as I am anyways.

I can tell you this much: I'm certainly not doing it. Today's not going to work for me. No matter how insistent and polite our neighbors and "business" partners have asked. My day is fucking booked.

Now Scooby knows that we can't send Alaska and Bones because I just instructed him to send Alaska and Bones out into the world hunting again for information from Brandon's sleazy junkball friends and acquaintances. Only this time it is in an official capacity. He also knows that I will pitch a fit if he himself offers to go. I need him here rallying the troops and mustering our forces and what not. All of this is said in silence in a matter of seconds between the two of us. It's amazing what two friends can convey to each other with shrugs and eyebrow raises and - in my case - grunts and groans.

"Okay," He nods finally and stops stroking his beard. "Handsome can you handle the Canucks?"

"Of course I can…"

"I'm black." Scooby and I finish for our predictable friend. Once I go back to my thousand-yard stare Scooby turns to Handsome and very seriously asks him to get it done "With no muss or fuss got it?" Handsome nods and smiles happily. He slaps a mock salute before spinning on his heel and marching off.

"What are you going to do?" Scooby asks after Handsome has walked out of earshot. That's a good question. What am I going to do?

Something.

Anything.

Maybe something desperate and stupid.

Brando's mind was a bag of cats. He had the third world war written all over him. Who knew what was going on between him and the pipe? I'm not saying getting the once over from some Russian thugs was reason alone to push the red button, but maybe it was time to turn things up a bit. Desperate could be exactly what we needed right now.

"I'm going to find Tommy Twelve Toes."

Whoa. Maybe not that desperate.

AR Bennett

Track Ten: Pink Flag

Thomas Archibald Haney, also known as one Tommy Twelve Toes, is – or at this point I guess we can say was – the manager for Lake Effect in Affect and close consigliere to Brandon Lake. Purveyor of black bag band needs and main junk dealer to the stars of this small town. Whatever The Band of Brandon needed Twelve Toes was the man to go and get it. Guitars. Guns. Dry ice. Laser light shows. Women of the pole. And perhaps most importantly,

Junk.

Gear.

The Dragon.

Blue Magic.

China White.

Tommy Twelve Toes on top of being an often-underage flirting, show promoting, percentage taking, occasional business manager to Erie Pennsylvania's greatest export since General Electric was also the top dealer and personal dabbler of the Big H. Heroin. If there was a single person to point a finger to and put on trial for the corruption and possible death of the city's true first son and punk icon it was Tommy Fucking Twelve Toes.

Why is he called Tommy Twelve Toes?

I mean that feels a bit like a freebie, doesn't it? This isn't exactly complex arithmetic here. What was it I said way back in the beginning? Nicknames often follow physical traits? Tommy Twelve Toes is called Tommy Twelve Toes because he has two extra digits where normal people would only have ten. One additional for each foot to be precise.

Make sense?

I feel like you'd have gotten there in the end all on your lonesome, but just in case you're a bit like me and was the kid in the back studying skirt and not paying attention to whichever teacher is teaching whatever they taught I'll spell it out for ya.

We call him Tommy Twelve Toes because he has twelve toes.

That was easy.

What isn't going to be easy is finding the rat faced fucker. Tommy Twelve Toes has been underground for quite some time. Not deep underground like Brando. Not Deep Six. But in the wind. Gone to ground. On the lamb.

In hiding.

See all the local beat cops on the street, and some of the federal suits keeping a bird's eye satellite view of this corrupt city of ours, know one thing: They want to put Twelve Toes in a twenty-four to life. After all this time Nancy Reagan's War on Drugs is still warring. The DEA is still administrating and enforcing drugs. Think of the children. We must keep the filthy terrible troubling trips away from the fresh faced and bushy tails of the youth.

Speaking of youth.

There's the whole taking girls back to the bus thing. But she was like totally eighteen.

Like totally.

Tommy Twelve Toes gives bad boys like me and mine a bad name. Well, badder. Worse? Whatever. Point is he and I aren't chummy chums buddy buds. I can't just dial him up and pop over for a spot of conversation and cookies. Which means I need to go where Twelve Toes goes and get intel from someone Twelve Toes knows. Preferably someone I also know. Who is also easily accessible. And willing to talk to me.

AR Bennett

Maybe Colt is right. It's not what you know it's who you know.

Luckily, I know a lot of people in this underworld world of ours.

Unluckily this means that I have to go to the Crooked Eye, a bar that I am technically not supposed to go nor am I welcome back to. Most people wouldn't have Erie as top of mind as an up all night sort of town. Las Vegas. New York. LA. Erie, Pennsylvania? Not likely. But make no mistake this is a drinker's town. There're more bars per capita than any other town of a similar size. More bars than churches.

True story.

People from small cities with nothing better to do that find poetry at the bottom of a bottle is nothing unique. Happens all the time. Happens everywhere. What does make the 814 unique and slightly odd is the fact that if you were to look at the puritan history of this place you might be confused to see open all night establishments dotting the main strip.

See back in the way back PA was a Quaker paradise. The cross Atlantic retreat for the puritan pure who came here clutching bibles to escape the hot and happening sex scene in jolly old England. Perhaps the ladies in London were showing too much ankle? What they brought with them besides belt buckles on their hats was what would become known even now as "Blue Laws".

Things such as:

It is illegal to sell liquor – or maybe more oddly a horse/car – on Sundays.

It is illegal for taverns to stay open past 2AM if a certain portion of their sales comes from food.

It is illegal to pour more than x number of shots into a cocktail.

It is illegal to sleep in a refrigerator box.

That last one has no relevance on this conversation. I just thought it was weird. For a town that is built on strict beliefs and harsh laws restricting good times it sure does have a lot of places that don't adhere to any of that. At all.

The Crooked Eye is one of those places. Despite it being well past what would be legally considered last call I have no doubt that it will still be open and happening. Tucked away downtown this jewel of the dive scene is the emerging Mecca for all things loud and fast and heavy. It's more music venue than bar which is how it slides past those pesky regulations and city ordinances.

Turns out those puritan prissies had nothing to say about concert halls. So put that in your pipe and smoke it pilgrim. Gotta love a good loop hole.

This bar that isn't technically a bar is the type of place where you can feel the music before you can even see the neon sign out front. That rising and sweaty guitar riff. The steady thump of drums. The deep pulsating undertow of the bass. Screaming vocals. It all hits your chest like a sucker punch as soon as you turn down the dark and narrow alleyway that makes up the entrance.

True to form there is still a crowd milling about smoking cigarettes out front. Like I said there is no doubt that this place would still be open even at this hour.

I just hope that it is open to me.

All societies have rules. Even and especially underground and underworld ones. There is a certain order to things. Our own forms of regulations and ordinances. This keeps things from descending into full on anarchy. No one wins when it is well and truly dog eat dog. One of these rules is the rule of being 86'd.

AR Bennett

As in:

Off the menu. Out of stock. Kicked out. Persona non grata.

Not

Welcome.

Now there are two types of 86s. There's the throw up lime green beer all over the bar on St. Paddy's Day sort of 86 where you're asked to leave so that you can shower and come back tomorrow when you are slightly sober. And then there is the other one.

The one that I'm currently facing.

The lifetime ban 86. The wanted posters behind the bar, shoot on sight, sort of 86. The three strikes and you're out 86. You have to do something pretty terrible to earn yourself an 86 like that. Something like, just for example, punching a bouncer and inciting a teensy tiny itty-bitty riot before stealing – though I prefer borrowing – the bartender's car to flee the scene with her cousin riding shotgun. That old chestnut.

Fear and Loathing in Erie PA.

The American Dream.

The bouncer outside has his hands full. There is a gaggle of scene kids choking up the entrance. They are all waiting to get big *X*s stamped on the back of the hands. Their own scarlet letter if you will. Though I don't know why. It's not like they aren't just going to wash it off in the bathroom so they can drink with the band. I angle my approach and duck in behind a pair of tweens sporting neon pink mohawks the size of industrial ceiling fans.

Just another black t-shirt in a sea of black tees.

I'll stop wearing black when they make a darker color.

Inside the noise really hits you. The stage set to the back is hosting some confusing chimera of hip-hop and Norwegian death metal. It's not half bad. Loud. Angry. Heavy. I just prefer my tunes to have a bit more clarity when it comes to the lyrics. I like to hear the words. More than that. I like to understand the words. This crowd it seems could care less. They are packed against the stage like worshippers at an altar. Moving in rhythm to the rage that flows through them. Hands in the air to better find the holy spirit of the thrash metalcore scene.

It gives the place a back heavy sort of feel. The bar is basically empty as everyone here is packed into the mosh pit and moving totally entranced by the metal.

This is good. It gives me plenty of space to achieve why I'm here in the first place. Which is have a polite and civil conversation with the goth queen and highest esteem of the Crooked Eye herself.

"Well, well, well. If it isn't the patron saint of bar fights and bad breakups." She says as soon as she sees me holding out a twenty trying to get service. "Get the fuck out Saint."

Maybe civil and polite was a bit of a stretch. But at least I'm not shot through by the shotgun hidden under the bar on site. So, let's call that progress. Celebration in small wins.

"Hiya Nik. Long time."

"And I'd like to keep it that way." She calmly and casually reaches under the bar and puts the double barrel down with a heavy *thunk*.

She looks the same as she's always looked. Raven black hair that matches the mascara that matches the lipstick which then matches the nail polish. Any point that is prominent on her body, and there are several of note, there is the silver shine of a piercing. Everything single point.

AR Bennett

From top to bottom.

North to south.

Tattoos cover corpse white skin which gives her a much-needed splash of color.

What can I say? I was going through a bit of a phase at the time. A phase, judging by the way her jaw is set and the dark light of barely controlled rage behind her eyes, that she still hasn't gotten over. Or wishes had ended sooner. Or not happened at all.

"You're still mad then I take it?"

As a response she rests a black nailed hand on the sawed-off pistol grip of the scattergun and slides it over the scarred and chipped bar so that both barrels point my way.

Oh Nikki. It just wasn't meant to be between us love.

Nikki Sixxx and I go way back. Back to the way back when The Bad Bunch was just Bad Lads and beyond. Back in the prequel. When we were young. Rebels without causes. Thick as thieves. She's an OG. An original. One of the founding fathers – or in her case mothers – of the current lords of the Kelso Beach House. We have history is what I'm saying. There are whole tomes written and studied by historical preservationists detailing the rise and fall of Nikki Sixxx and I.

But then what had happened, happened and here we are. Her thrice pierced lip shaking with anger. Me staring down the dual barrels of a boomstick.

I'm suddenly hit with the feeling that maybe there is something to settling down. Maybe all this tail is tempting me down dark paths with consequences echoing through eternity. Maybe all these wounded hearts club members are taking me down the boulevard of broken dreams. Find myself a nice girl. Someone outside The Life.

Maybe a nurse or something?

I've always felt if a woman can pull off scrubs, she can look sexy in anything.

There are no loaded guns pointed at faces behind white picket fences and his and her towels. No vendettas. No flashed thoughts flickering through my mind of sucking chest wounds and pink mist decorated bar stools. Just brunches and weekend trips to Home Depot if there's time. Could be nice.

Of course there's the flip side of that coin. That sinking feeling slithering around in my cerebellum. That maybe

Just maybe

It's not them that's the problem. I'm coming to terms with the fact that it very well could be me. Now that's a thought, isn't it?

Shrinks and couches can wait.

The sand in the hourglass is running thin and I can always come to terms with myself later. Providing of course I'm still above ground in the sunshine and not pushing daisies by then. I hold my hands up in surrender. Waving the white flag as it were. With a smile I slide slightly further down the bar away from both barrels which seem to be slowly tracking me. At this range, it won't even matter. Both shells right in the ten ring.

Bullseye.

Blood splatters crimson and my lungs add to the décor along with the scattered bras and stapled dollar bills covered in graffiti that line the walls.

"Fair enough. I'm gone. Outta your hair and on my way. Right after I get a bit of your help."

Oblivious to our little drama the band rages on in the background. Heavy. Hard. Animalistic. Which suits her mood just fine. There are worse soundtracks to score the end of the world to, I guess.

"You need my help?" She snarls. Black lips curl over bared teeth. Finger caressing trigger. "That's rich. Coming from you. I needed you once. You know that?"

"I do and you did."

"And what did you do?"

"What I did."

There's that tense moment milliseconds before death when all the greatest hits of your misguided life come rushing back. A montage of memorable moments that gets you thinking that it's looking more and more probable that your heart is going to be heavier than a feather. She stares me down. Dark eyes probing and searching my baby blues. If this is the end, the least I can do is hold her gaze.

What the hell. It's not like I planned on dying in bed anyways. Better to see it coming. Meet it head on.

Time is doing that thing where it is not behaving as it should. Seconds stretch like taffy into minutes into hours into eternity. Finally, she sighs and slides the shotgun back under the bar.

"Ever heard of the scorpion and the frog Saint?" She asks when she comes back up.

"I don't really go in for folk music."

She shakes her head. I shrug sheepishly. What can you do? What's done is done. Time marches on and problems only are problems as long as new ones haven't popped up.

"Okay. You're not worth the chair. So, what do you want?"

"I need your help Nik."

"You said that already. What I am failing to see is what does your little deals with devils have to do with me?"

Grapevines and gossip. Small towns with nothing better to do than share the tea. In a life like ours, close-knit community chatter is like currency. Extra extra. Read all about it.

"So, you've heard? Does everyone know?"

"Everyone who's anyone. You're hot news. More press than a release. The streets are alive with the sounds of your dark dealings. You never struck me as a communist Saint. Too self-serving."

Of course everyone knew. We criminals are a bunch of chatty Kathys. Worse than grandmothers at bridge games. All crime is connected it seems. I take her jabs on the chin because it is better than taking buckshot to the chest. Call me a commie. Call me self-serving. Egotistical. Narcissistic. Paint me in any unfavorable brush you want. I had my reasons and I did what I did.

"Well, the fact you have your ear to the wire and all the headlines flow through you is exactly what I need right now. I just need to find Tommy, Nik. Those who know know, and you're one of those."

"Tommy Twelve Toes?"

"The one and the same."

She doesn't answer. Not right away. Instead, she reaches down to the very bottom most shelf and pulls up a bottle of whiskey. She sets two chipped classes on the bar and pours the gasoline-colored hooch into both. Before sliding mine over to me she pauses, grabs a bottle of hellfire hot sauce, and shakes in a rather unhealthy dose. Then bone white fingers covered in colorful tattoos push it my way. That's fair. I probably deserved that.

I raise my glass and she raises hers. Cheers.

To breaking and mending fences maybe.

As soon as the concoction touches my tongue, red alarm bells begin flashing in my brain. Words in big white block letters dance through my mind.

AR Bennett

Danger.

Napalm.

Searing flesh.

Jungles in Vietnam.

Liquid fire leaks from my broken nose while smoke and steam escape from my ears. If I wasn't awake before what with all the adrenaline of crimes incomplete, fist fights fought, and coke snorted, I was certainly up and at 'em now. Jesus Christ. As far as peace offerings go this wasn't. I cough and wheeze and wipe the burning hell off my lips with the back of my hand. There's the glimmer of a faint smile on her black lips.

At least someone is enjoying this.

"Tell me Saint. Is your little caper cinema?" She asks when my coughing and choking subsides.

Everyone has their kinks. Hers is classic cinema. She loses herself in film. Loves it. The older the better. Proper film. Casablanca. Maltese Falcon. The Man Who Wasn't There. Chinatown. If your pockets are filled with nothing but sand a good story can be considered currency.

If that story just so happened to paint me as a proper idiot and put me in a bad light than all the better. That's just gold. Mastercard quality scratch accepted everywhere.

"Could we just not this time?"

"We could and then you could get the fuck out."

Fine.

This is fine.

Why not? Not like my life is on the line here or anything. Clocks tick and tock as time moves on. Tempus Fugit.

Time flies.

She'll want it in 35mm. Golden Age. 1.37:1. Academy ratio. Black and white obviously. Okay. If that's how it has to be then that's how it's got to be.

The bar seems to freeze. Just for a second. A brief moment in time when nothing moves. Not the whiskey glass brought to her lips. Not the band caught in mid motion or the mosh pit in mid mosh. The sound fades. The bar flies flutter in ultra stylized slow motion that allows you to see the individual wings slowly flapping.

Then suddenly everything starts to move backwards. Slowly at first. The whiskey pours back up into the bottle from the glasses. Nikki Sixxx moves about in retrograde. I sit on the barstool for a moment and watch as the world rewinds. Getting up I begin to walk forward through a backward world. Outside the bar the scene kids go back to the bouncer and big black *X*s disappear back up into a permanent marker off their hands. Cigarettes are extinguished as lighter flames flicker out and are put back into packs.

Outside of the alley cars stop at green lights and move backwards at red. Above even the moon moves against its normal rhythm. Birds fly backwards. The streets start to liven up as more and more people walk backwards into bars where they find their drinks reappearing and refilling. The hustle and bustle of a drinking town comes alive.

I walk down the sidewalks and streets against the flow. Each step forward brings me one step back. Yachts come un-collided. Party guests walk off the gangplank and back to the gate to have invitations handed back to them by guards with guns.

The sun rises in the west and starts its course to set in the east.

As I walk the color starts to drain from my skin. First with my fingertips and then my hands then up

AR Bennett

my arms. I watch as the tan of a summer sun spent outdoors and on the water bleaches away to a crisp film like gray. By the time I'm back at the Kelso Beach House to watch the day play out in reverse there are no colors left in the world other than crisp shades of black and white.

    As I walk through The Bad Bunch who are oblivious to my presence and are going about their day opposite to how time works, I spy a faded fedora resting next to a head down barfly at the bar. I snag it as I move back to the office where I sit down in the duct taped office chair and put my feet up on the desk.

    The fedora goes on my head and I watch the world play out backwards as more and more color leaches out of life around me. Things pick up speed until it is all just a blur of motion falling in reverse. I lean back. Let it play out. Pull the fedora down over my eyes and wait until the rapidly increasing movement blends together and the whole world seems to

FADE OUT

TWO DAYS EARLIER

AR Bennett

FADE IN

I push the fedora back and open my eyes. The backroom of the beach house has morphed into a cluttered office fit for a private detective. A typewriter rests on the corner of my desk. Printed pictures sit in stacks. Gone is my t-shirt and boardshorts. Replaced by a pin striped suit and loosely knotted tie.

I pull a Lucky Strike from a silver case in my breast pocket and strike a match to light it. Unfiltered tobacco fills my lungs and streams out my unbroken nose. Looking around I can immediately tell this is the realm of noir. The world of the Big Eight Studios. Birthplace of Kurosawa. Of Lang, Wilder, Lupino, Dassin and Welles. Stark and dramatic lighting. Hyper expressive. Exaggerated costumes. Overstated themes and motifs.

Underlying existentialist philosophy.

Shadow becomes a character of its own.

Which is why I am seated behind my desk with my feet up partially cast in one. The morally ambiguous protagonist literally shaded between light and dark. The camera is sharply angled and distorted with an asymmetrical flair.

Outside the open window there is the hum of a hustling and bustling cityscape. New York or LA maybe. Somewhere definitely not my strip of quiet and secluded beach front. You can practically taste the dark alleyways and crime happening within them. It's night because it has to be.

These things usually are narrated, aren't they? Guess I should be getting to it then.

I loosen my tie a bit further and clear my throat. Then the soundtrack is laid in and over the film.

THE BAD BUNCH

This whole stinking town has been in the grips of heatwave all summer. It hadn't rained a day. The heat was all the radio could talk about. The only thing the newsies would type about.

The Heat.

Heat makes a man do crazy things. Things often against his better nature. And this summer we've all been cooking in it. People were starting to go mad. Fray around the edges. The lines between right and wrong, good and evil, had begun to blur into vapors coming off the sizzling streets.

It's the type of night you want nothing more than to curl up into a cold stiff drink but you can't because the ice cubes have long since melted. You take one anyway. That's how you know it's hot. When the burn of the bourbon actually cools you down. Bad news for the bottles. Bad news for the beat cops out on the streets too. That false cool gets everyone so heated, blood boiling behind the booze, that you could flick a smoke and this whole steaming city would go up in flames.

It's a tinder box out there.

I'd just come back from a hard time up town. The sort of thing that warrants putting on one of the two suits hanging in my closet. The black one. A funeral for a friend. In this heat it just didn't feel right. Nothing did.

Funerals don't feel like funerals without rain.

They don't feel like funerals without a stiff either.

Bad enough that we had to be all gathered together under this baking sun. But to be gathered all together under the baking sun only to watch an empty casket get lowered into the dry brown ground? That's not how these things ought to go.

And it is a gathering. All the old faces.

Some new ones too.

That's where I first saw her. Wrapped in the black of mourning. Entirely shaded under an umbrella held tight to her shoulder to not let a single ray of sunlight in. Sunglasses big enough to cover damp eyes. Or maybe they were there to hide bone dry cheeks about as wet as the ground we gathered around.

There's no real way of knowing.

But I know this, even in a crowd of trouble she looked the most. I knew that much from the very beginning. Something about the way she carried herself that stood out against the riff raff and shadowy faces. A dark light in the dim underworld that made up this crowd. A beacon in a deeper darker black than all those shades of gray.

In my line of work, you get pretty good at reading people. And this one might as well been a sign written in big advertising block letters. But what do I know? I'm just a small-town dick...

*****

"That's true." Nikki Sixxx interrupts and the whole world is thrust back into the now and the real. I need to blink the bright lights of living technicolor out of my eyes.

"I know I deserved that, but if I could continue that would be great."

"I just wanted it on the record that you're a small-town dick."

"Detective. A small-town *detective*. It's the lingo of the time."

Can't do noir without the lingo. Have to set the tone and dress the stage. That said I did leave myself fairly wide open for that one I had to be honest. Still this story isn't going to tell itself.

"Could I?"

She waves a hand dismissively. The world fades back to gray.

*****

If you look closely at the upper right-hand corner of the screen you can see an orange and yellow ring flash there. Blink and you'll miss it. In the industry we call these "cigarette burns". They mark the transition of one reel of film to another.

Where were we?

Oh yeah.

But what do I know? I'm just a small-town *detective* working all the cases no one wants to touch with a ten-foot pole. It's a hard gig being down in the dirt, down in the muck and mire and filth of this filthy city, but somebody's got to do it.

And that somebody is me.

It pays the bills.

Hard gigs like the ones I'm used to can teach you a thing or two about the world and the people within it. Everybody wants something. Sure, they are all here to pay respects to the missing and presumed dead, but that doesn't mean that's all they want.

It's not apparent then what she wants. But I can tell it's coming.

There are more respects paid than what the dead man deserved. More tears shed than what were owed. Even still I'm last to leave the cemetery. Last one standing looking down into an empty hole rapidly filling with dirt.

I light a Lucky and blow smoke rings into the all too bright sky as I watch her slide into a big black car. The driver holds the door for her. She seems to move from shadow to shadow by folding herself in elegantly until she disappears behind tinted glass windows.

AR Bennett

I'm thinking of her long legs flashing briefly in the sweltering sun, head back fedora tilted over my eyes, when there's a knock at my door to my office. I tilt the fedora up and call for them to come in.

"I'm heading home for the night boss." My secretary pops her head in. She's wearing the flapper attire that has still stayed in fashion despite the 20s having stopped roaring. It's a hard look to pull off and I'm not so sure Scooby can manage it.

*****

Outside the narrative I can hear Nikki tsking in disapproval. She feels a type of way that I've cast Scoob as my diminutive secretary. He was her friend once too. But what am I going to do? It's not like I'm putting Alaska in that dress.

*****

"Go ahead doll. These cold cases will keep till morning."

She closes the door and leaves me alone to my own thoughts. The ceiling fan spins slowly overhead creating eddies of smoke circles that drift and float upward. I pour that drink. From a locked drawer in my desk, I pull out a case that is more personal than professional.

The disappearance of the Cabana Club's lead act.

Noone can seem to crack this one yet.

Which leaves me to look into it. See I've got a connection with the missing. We came up together. This one won't pay the bills but it might help me sleep at night. The file isn't much to go on. It's a newspaper clipping with a headline in big bold print that simply reads "MISSING PRESUMED DEAD." A photo of a boat. Some scribbled notes I've managed to put together. It's thin. But it has the feeling that if I dive into this one, I'm diving into trouble.

Then my door opens again and I look up to see standing in the shadows that trouble has found me already.

"I hear you're the man to know if you're looking to find things." Comes the exotic and vaguely foreign voice. Silken honey dipped in sex and sin. Caviar and chilled vodka.

"Depends on what needs being found."

I'm not being discreet about the fact my hand is not so subtly on the butt of my .45 holstered to my side. I've made a lot of enemies in this town and you never know who is going to walk through your door looking for their fair shake. She steps into the light in a way that is more glide than step. That dress goes on for long enough to show that her legs go on for days further. Smoke curls around her thin lips. The lit cigarette held in her teeth with a long and thin opera length holder. Despite the heat the room seems to get a bit colder.

"I'm looking for an album."

"Then I recommend Graham's Vinyls."

Long heels click on broken tiles as she struts further into my office. The red bottoms of her shoes match her nail polish which matches her lipstick. Crimson and provocative. Barely kept promises of pleasure. And blood.

Nothing about her comes from the five and dime. Posh. Sophisticated. From the way she dresses to the way she moves to the way she holds her smoke.

"It's not that type of album." She says when she has glided up against the edge of my desk. "And you won't be needing that. 1911, is it?"

She knows her guns. This isn't a surprise to me. She seems the type. I am a bit surprised when she sits down on the corner of my desk and the moonlight bounces off her skin. This is a practiced pose. Designed to get what she wants from who she wants. I know right then and there it's trouble.

Course there's knowing what you know in the cool and calm and then knowing what you know in the heat. Hesitantly I slide my hand off the butt of my gun.

"Aren't you going to offer me a drink?" She asks with a slight chin nod towards the open bottle on my desk.

"Do you want a drink Miss…?"

"Alisa." She nods as I pour the amber liquid into another glass and push it her way. The look on her face as she slowly sips it is as someone more accustomed to top shelf stuff but raised too proper and polite to say anything. "You can all me Ali."

"So, Miss Ali…"

"Just Ali."

"…So, Ali, what's this about an album?"

She pauses to sip her drink. Her eyes linger on mine for a brief moment that's no doubt going to spell my downfall. She's got this type of beauty that makes a guy think he could make it stay if he took his own life. Miss Murder. All silk and smooth spider webs to the fly. The bright plumage of toxic flowers that adapt poison as their survival mechanism of choice. Exotic. Dangerous. Enthralling.

I've heard this song before. I'm not so sure I like the tune. I should end it right here. Say I'm not her man. Not the guy with the good nose for finding what can't be found. Show her the door. But then there's the dress and the heat and the smoke slowly creeping toward the ceiling in slow motion.

Maybe the song can't be all that bad. Sure, I've heard it before but maybe this time it'll be different.

Play it again Sam.

"How familiar are you with Brandon Lake? The lead act at the Cabana Club?"

Empty coffins lowered under brown grass. Umbrellas for shade and sunglasses to hide dangerous eyes. She knows I know. No doubt saw me standing there the same way I saw her.

So why the act?

"Cut the bull doll. You know I do. You were there, same as me. At the cemetery. Or did you think I wouldn't notice?"

A faint smile. The upward twitch of a cat who cornered a mouse.

"I was hoping you'd notice."

"Yeah, and why's that?"

She finishes her drink and sets the glass softly down on my desk. Nails tap the crystal with a faint beat I know I've heard before but can't place. She has this bemused look on her face that tells me she has a feeling that all of this is simply a game being played.

"Because like I said you are the man to know. I've heard all about you Mr. Saint. Have a knack for opportunity and got your fingers in a lot of pies. You seem to know everyone but have no allegiance to anyone. Born on the outs as it were. A guy who can go into places he shouldn't and get things others can't. That makes you resourceful. I like resourceful."

"Oh shucks. You're making me blush."

"You sure that's from the compliment?" She smiles dangerously. A cat's smile. Coy and fitting for her tight face and tighter features. She readjusts on the desk and there is a flash of athletic thigh, a dancer's thigh, before fading back under expensive silken threads. Smiles again seeing that I've seen. "To business, yes?"

I nod.

Sure. Let's keep it at that.

"You see before Brandon Lake went missing…"

"…And is presumed dead."

"Da. Before Brandon went missing and was presumed dead he finished one last body of work. An album. His final masterpiece. A new noise that will change the shape of punk to come."

That makes sense. Knowing Brandon, I could see him banging out one last fuck you to the world before shuffling off this mortal coil. That all tracks. What doesn't track is how would this prim and proper princess in her expensive heels and polite and polished exterior know about it?

"You know this how exactly?"

She smiles. A dark Cheshire Cat grin that catches the moonlight. The tapping on the glass continues to the tune I know I know but still can't for the life of me put a song to in my mind.

"Because I was there."

"You were?"

"Da. I was." There is this brief dark shadow that passes over her porcelain complexion. Regret? Remorse? It fades too quickly to know for certain. "We had a…special connection Brandon and I. A shared love of rebellion if you will."

"Sure." I'm not some rube off an Okie truck. I've been around the block more times than I can tell. Despite what her sad eyes are telling me I can see the lie behind the crocodile tears. "Let's say that I believe that little bit of theater. Three's still a crowd doll. And everyone knows Brandon Lake's primary partner was the pipe. So, unless you had a shared love of that, I'm thinking everything you're saying amounts to a hill of beans."

"He had his vices. You do too do you not? Canadian friends to keep happy? Addicted to the dark deals, no?" Her response wasn't as cold as I had expected. There seems to be some genuine anger hidden under the frigid and calculated surface. "But these things, that was what made him who he was. Do you know what happens when a person of renown goes missing? And is presumed dead?"

"Yeah, they disappear."

She laughs. Rolls her eyes. Whatever hidden agenda or lingering sentiment is now, back again, under the porcelain surface of the mask she keeps as a face. "No, what I mean is do you know what happens next?"

I did. There's the beat on the street and dogs in the woods. Sniffing about. Cold cases don't win re-election campaigns. Bad for records. Bad for justice. Makes the powers that be look incompetent. Also makes the powers that aren't show some true colors. Blood in the water and the scavengers start circling. She can tell by my nod that I know what she is saying. That I'm inline and tracking.

"I merely want to make sure this final brilliant work of art, made from someone who…who I cared for…deeply," there's that flicker of emotion again. The slight stumble over words. The quiver of a bottom lip. I'm sure she'd like to thank the Academy. "doesn't fall into the wrong hands."

"Only that it falls into your hands then?"

"Da, I want to safeguard his vision. Make sure it receives the treatment it deserves. Treatment aligned with his wishes."

How very noble.

How very trite.

Suckers are born every day. Credit where credit is due though, whatever she is selling she sure is good at it. I almost started to believe it for a moment. Course I'm a sucker for a damsel in distress. She knows just how to play it. Just how to bait the hook and get me to bite.

I'm about to turn her away. Wash my hands of this whole business and go back to the bottle until this whole crooked night fades away. Then it hits me.

Like a .45 to the chest.

A sudden and sharp realization.

That tune? Tapped on glass by crimson nails? I know where I know it from. It's an unreleased single from Lake Effect's last album. Never saw the light of day. Was never recorded or distributed. A bit of fooling around and messing about. Only someone who'd been there, who'd known Brandon enough that he would have trusted them, would be familiar.

"Okay," I take the fedora off a sweat dripped forehead and set it on top of my desk. On top of the file I was studying. "Let's say I believe you. And I'm not saying I do. But say I did. Where'd you have me start?"

Shit. That smile? That one was real. Step into my parlor said the spider to the fly. As the sounds of the night intensify outside the window, she spells out her request. Fills in the details. The more she talks the more I'm finding it hard to pay attention. Alabaster thighs under silken threads. The sharp and articulated lines of a former ballerina.

By the time she's done, off my desk and sliding a thick envelope out of her clutch, she's got me wrapped around her finger. The trap is set. I can feel the line pull tight.

"Thank you for the drink, Mr. Saint." She says and pushes the envelope over my desk to me. It doesn't take a detective to know that it's heavy with cash. "I knew you'd be the man for this job. I just hope you can get it done soon. I'm afraid I'm not the only interested party."

I tuck the envelope into my suit pocket and stand from my chair. This is a dangerous play. I know that. But I wouldn't be me if I didn't take the gamble.

"I'll get it done." I say. Then without thinking, without consideration, I leap before I look. "How about another drink?"

*****

There's this wobbling and burning on the screen as the film fails and the projector clicks off. I shake off the last remaining shadows and work living color back into my fingers. The real world comes into clarity just in time for me to see Nikki's disapproval etched across her face.

"You're an idiot." She says as the band finishes up a set. The lights are rising. Closing time. "A bit of skirt and some flirt and you fall, head over heels, into the arms of the Russian Reaper. For what? A good time? One night stand? Come on Saint."

She's not wrong. A bit oversimplified but yeah. Not wrong. The crowd in front of the stage start to disperse. Make their way back to the bar. I'm still no closer to my goal than I was when I came in.

"Why not give the money back? Tell your new boo you came up with jack. Sorry for the inconvenience. Here's your ruples. Better luck with the next sucker."

"Well…"

"Well?" She asks. There's not much to say that a sheepish shrug can't convey. It takes her just half a second to get my drift. "You don't have it."

"I do not."

"You've already spent it. Jesus Christ on toast." Nikki laughs. There is an almost I-told-you-so underlining quality to her chuckle. A sadness that comes as no surprise to her because she already saw it coming. She knows my nature. She was there when it was formed. "What does that type of change buy these days?"

"Not as much as I'd like. Councilmen on zoning committees aren't cheap it turns out."

"Of course." She shakes her head. "That damn beach house. Your one true love."

"The one and the same. What won't we do for love?"

"I can't believe I loved you once."

That she did. Put her trust in me and stood by my side. And I burned it all down.

"If you did once then do it for that. Look Nik, I need your help. I need to find Tommy. He's the best chance I got to get the good times back on track. Get out from under this. I'm basically begging here. Please? For old times? For The Bad Bunch?"

She pours another drink. Just one this time. None for me. Not even with hot sauce as a chaser. I can tell she is struggling. Conflicted. On one hand I'm sure she'd probably enjoy seeing me get deep sixed. After everything I'm not sure if I'd blame her.

But on the other hand,

On the other hand, she was one of us. Once. The Kelso Beach house had a bit of her sweat and some of her tears in its woodwork. Sure, I needed to pay the piper, and someday I just might, but what of the rest of the bunch? They were her friends too once. Should they all go down for me?

Bad for the goose is bad for the gander?

I let her think it over. I've done enough talking. The clock keeps ticking though. And with each tock

I'm getting closer to a deadline that might be just that.

A

Dead

Line.

Finally, she knocks back the shot and sets it aside. Her dark eyes are full of hurt and heartache and perhaps most importantly a bit of determination. Guess she's made up her mind. My little cinema, stylized and her type of kink, made me look like a proper idiot. And to her that's a high bar no doubt. It certainly didn't mend any fences or make up for what I did.

Riots. GTA. Affairs with cousins.

Bit of this. Bit of that. Ancient histories.

But it might be enough to buy some goodwill for The Bunch. That's what I'm hoping anyways. Who knows though. Could have been a waste of time. Maybe just a way to get some backstory off my chest. Keep everyone honest and on track. There's always that. Could be that now was as good of time as any for some exposition ya know?

She sighs. Shakes her head in sad defeat.

"You really are the patron saint of getting your way no matter the costs, aren't you?"

I nod. Sure, seems to sum it up from where I'm sitting. Doesn't mean I'm happy about it, just that I see no point in arguing. When she's right she's right.

"Tommy Twelve Toes has been ran out and run dry of every dive from here to Fairview. He's burned every friendly barstool and earned his way into all of his 86s. He needs to travel far and wide to source and sell his junk and it's only a matter of time before he's kicked out of there too."

That sounds like Tommy. I nod for Nikki to go on.

"Where do you go when no bar in the city will pour you? Not even mine and not even yours? You go where all desperados go. Down. Erie might be closed off to Twelve Toes, but Edinboro isn't. He's found safe harbor with the college kids at the Copper Coin. I believe you know it?"

Yeah. I know it. And it's not what I'm hoping to hear.

"I'm sure The Twins will be very happy to see you. You just can't help yourself but burn it all down can you Saint?" She laughs. This time she means it and finds the idea genuinely funny. "I'd pay money to be there when those two show you just how happy they are. Now you got what you came for. A heading and a bearing. Now, get the fuck out of my bar."

She motions for a bouncer to come over and the big guy appears behind me. He grabs a shoulder and I'm lifted out of the stool. This guy has put in the time at the bench press. He's managed to manhandle me without even so much as batting an eye.

"Thank you, Nik." I say as I'm being hauled away.

"I didn't do it for you."

She waves her hand and the big dude continues hauling me off. Gets me to the door and without much muss or fuss pitches me into the rapidly fading night.

Track Eleven: Never Mind The Bollocks

I've been spending a lot of time face down on the ground this evening.

The bouncer pitches me out in a manner that suggests he should have probably gone pro. Gone State at the very least. I lay there in the alley amidst the discarded cigarette butts and collect my thoughts. Process what needs processing.

This feels a bit like nowhere. Like I went one step forward only to have been thrown two steps back. A much to do about nothing. There's that voice in the back of my head that asks if I've gone enough rounds. That, maybe, I should just stay down.

Maybe.

I am and have done a great number of things.

I play and have been played by the sex game. Spoken in silver tongues and charmed my way as a conman. Thrown a few beatings and received my fair share. I might be one of a few people who know the edge and haven't yet gone over. Dabbled in this. Traded in that.

But one thing that I won't do.

Have never done and will never do.

Is be a quitter.

I pick myself up from the sidewalk and shake some dignity back into my bones. There's still some dog left in this fight. After all this won't be the first time I've been thrown out of a bar – this bar to be precise – and it will no doubt not be the last.

Unless that is if I fail to get this tape.

AR Bennett

Here's hoping you can't get 86'd from a bar in heaven.

Right. Heaven. Who am I kidding?

At least I have a scent. A trail to follow. Tommy Twelve Toes isn't dead in a ditch just yet. He isn't down in Mexico. Not all tengo doce dedos down south of the border and beyond my reach. Edinboro is less than ideal. I would have happily taken Pittsburgh or even fucking Cleveland if that were the case. But I didn't have time for Pittsburgh or Cleveland. I barely had time for Edinboro.

Somewhere over the horizon the sun started waking up. The night sky turned a deep dark blue. Darkest before the dawn. Soon the first rays of sunlight would tear through the sky and turn that royal blue into hues of pinks and yellows and fiery oranges.

Time waits for no man.

I'm not making it to the Boro on foot. I'll need wheels which means I'll need Scooby. I put feet to street and start heading back the way I came. Backtracking feels bad when you're on a running clock. I've been here and done this before. Gives me time to think though.

Think about the mess I'm in and how I got here. Letting my worse impulses get the better of me. Spinning in circles. All the same scenes just with different characters and settings. Worst part is I'm still not sure what it's all for.

I have an idea.

A glimmer of understanding. Pieces of the puzzle are put in place here and there, but I still have no clue what the image on the box looks like. I might have lost the forest through the trees. I know Mikhailov wants the tape. Was willing to pay big money to get it. I know she'd tried before but her goons came up empty handed.

Why she wants it?

Don't know.

The only theory is she wants it because of exactly why she said she did. She was there when it was recorded. Somehow, she doesn't strike me as the sentimental type though. Then there's Colt. What's his role in this?

The city is finally starting to calm down as the sun comes up. Only the stoutest of drunks wobble down the streets towards homes unknown. The whole city is put under a blanket of calm even if for just the briefest of moments. The reverse circadian rhythm of a late-night town come dawn. Over the lake the light starts to change to a thick red.

This night had bled away.

Nothing about this morning told me that the bleeding would stop anytime soon. Red skies in morning sailors take warning and all that.

As I walk my gut tells me Colt has his hand in this too. After all he has his fingers in a lot of pies. Sure, he could have just gotten drunk and pirated his own yacht. He could have just taken her out and by happenstance hit the precise boat containing the precise thing I currently needed. In crime there is always coincidence.

Sure. Maybe.

But that didn't feel right, now did it? He's got to be involved somehow. Right?

I'm head down spinning my wheels when I come around a corner and realize I might just get an opportunity to get an answer to that.

As if on cue a pack of men in fashionable and expensive suits step out of the shadows and materialize in front of me. A sleek black vehicle that is old enough to be considered an automobile and not a car pulls out of an alley and cuts off my path. Two goons get out of the back and stand arms crossed as further deterrent.

Something about them just screamed cop.

Or worse yet.

Ex-cop.

Turned hired gun. The badges are gone but the swagger remains. Not many people in this city had the means to fund a private security force made up of former troopers and dicks (Man the noir thing sticks with you for a bit, doesn't it? Hard to get off the tongue).

In fact, the list was pretty damn close to just one.

"Look, if you're going to cite me for drinking in public, I'll have you know that I was drinking in a bar and they threw me into public."

The goons say nothing. They are not being paid to talk or to smile or smirk at borrowed jokes. Out from behind the big bold antique sedan slithers out someone who wouldn't you know it I don't really want to see slithering about.

Fuck.

Well, that's one theory all but confirmed.

I nod my head and smile the smile of a man who is only doing it because it's in his nature to do so. The devil may care. You know the type.

"Charlie."

"Saint."

Charlie comes around the car and he's all smiles in his posh suit. Two buttons and a vest. Something straight out of gangster GQ. It's a fitting look for the right-hand man of the devil himself. I motion my chin to his men.

"See you brought your biggest gorillas with you."

The goons are actually rather diminutive. Angry in the way small dogs are always angry or how Napoleon was angry. Charlie chuckles.

"More than enough for you Saint."

He's probably right. Just because they were tiny tykes playing dress up in their gangster daddy's clothes didn't make them any less dangerous. You know chihuahuas cause more injuries than pitbulls?

"You're right Charlie. It has been a night."

"That it has. Might we have a word?"

I look from Charlie to the two goons to the big black Rolls Royce and back to Charlie. None of this feels very friendly chat like.

"Just a word?"

To make my initial assessment even clearer the tiny terrors crack their knuckles and stretch their arms in a manner that in no way discretely shows off guns in holsters concealed under suit coats. Makes for a rather convincing argument.

Charlie gives his guys a head nod and they get to it. Two goons to either side. Rough hands under my arms as they drag me to the car. My low-top Converse sneakers are left to scrape on the sidewalk. The trunk of the Rolls pops open and the dynamic duo pull me that way.

"Oh, come on guys. Not the trunk. It's not like I don't know where we're going anyways."

"Sorry Saint." Charlie shrugs. "He insisted."

"Well then at least let me get in on my own?"

It's possible I can salvage some dignity out of this. Possible. Not probable. The goons surely don't seem to think so. They hoist me up and crumple me into the boot without a second thought or even the faintest pause. I'm crammed in against the rich Corinthian Leather as if I was a bit of luggage. Standing over me and taking up all the faint rays of the rising sun Charlie smiles his little Charlie smile and puts his hands on the trunk lid.

"Comfy?"

AR Bennett

"Not particularly no."

"Good."

He slams the trunk shut leaving me cramped up alone in the dark confines. Truth be told it's not half bad actually. Sort of cozy in a way. If you can get past the claustrophobia that is. As the Rolls started to pull out, I find myself drifting off.

I had this friend who went to the sandbox. He'd used to say that the key to surviving a situation that was beyond your control was to get your sleep in when, and where, you can. Not bad advice that.

Course, he did go crazy and holed himself up somewhere in the Canadian wilderness. Locked in a cabin full of guns and mason jars to piss in. So maybe take that with a grain of salt or two.

Still. There could be worse places to catch some much-needed Zs. As soon as I feel the big old car get underway and, on the road, the deep dark of a confined space and the soft leather against my cheek has my eyes getting heavy. Hard to keep open. Soon they are closed entirely.

I sleep.

And then I dream.

Track Twelve: Interlude

Wild nights equate to even wilder dreams.
There is a sense that I'm moving, floating, feather light and adrift through the darkness of time and space. Half-forgotten punk songs play through the ether. A kaleidoscope of colors and scents and thoughts fills up the space between spaces. Nowhere. And everywhere.

Then the fog lifts and I'm back at the Kelso Beach House.

At.

Not in.

Because at this point in time there was no way in. It's boarded up. Abandoned. Dark and mysterious and closed off to wayward souls or prying eyes.

Is this a dream or a memory?

"Why not both?"

I look to my left and there is Younger Me standing on the big wrap around porch that faces the lake. He's swinging a crowbar in one hand, an open bottle of something vaguely resembling whiskey swings in the other. Too young to get the good stuff. Too broke to have someone get it even if he could.

"Do you see this as the beginning," he asks still swinging the crowbar. There's that dream feeling of having someone see you without anyone being there to have seen. "Or is this the end?"

Young eyes fresh and new and hot with rebellion look through me.

Past me.

I shrug in the way someone with no physical body can shrug. Ethereal. Not really here. That's fine by me. Just like back up in the waking world I can be taken somewhere without doing the driving. It's hard to speak with no mouth so I let my eyes do the talking. He'll know what I mean. they are his eyes too. Or will be.

I tell him don't worry about me. Pay me no mind. Just visiting. It's his party he can do with it what he will. I am just

Along for the ride.

"Okay then." He smiles. Lifts up the big metal tool. "Let's do this."

"This is a terrible idea."

"Ruh roh gang…Scaredy Scooby is here again."

Scooby crosses his arms over his chest in protest. He's got a cast on his right arm, which incidentally matches the cast I've got on my left. One for the guy in the driver's seat. One for the guy in the passenger's seat.

"I'm not scared Saint. I'm just saying this is a bad idea. We are crossing a line here man."

He's not wrong. This is a little above and beyond from our normal brand of rebellious revelry. But it just has to be done. I mean, would you just look at it? This beautiful old probably haunted as shit place just sitting here on this secluded spot of beach and we are what? Regulated to squat on the porch?

Not tonight.

Not anymore.

That's what the crowbar is for. I mean…what else are crowbars for? This place has sat here, just out of reach from kids like us for what had to be generations. The class of hooligans before us and those before them. If you came up this way in these parts there was a strong chance you would have had a night or two on the sandy overgrown front lawn and porch of the fabled Kelso Beach House.

Our dad's dads probably too.

And not once in all that time had someone thought to pry it open. Bring a crowbar down to the beach and let some fresh air in. Come on folks. Are we bad boys or what?

Just can't resist. My voice echoes through the ether. I've got my popcorn and I'm enjoying the show. Red and blue 3D glasses perched on my broken nose. The kind that they give at theaters and are meant to be chucked in the bin when the credits roll.

Down by the bonfire sparked up in the sand that provides just enough light for some casual destruction of private property and possible breaking and entering an acoustic guitar starts playing softly. I set my popcorn down and leave Younger Me to prying off plywood sheets and two by fours.

Floating over the sand. Carried on by phantom notes that drift and swirl through the warm summer air. A group of younger teens sit in a circle around the fire. Mostly girls. Some guys too. All of them drawn into the sound.

He was good even back then.

Destiny echoes off those cords. A calling. A dream and a demise.

I listen to the music and watch as the shadowed figure at the center of the fire circle starts to really get into it. Carried away by it. When he is finished one of the girls in the circle, stars in her eyes and breath caught on her tongue, asks "What do you call that song?"

The shadowy figure sets his guitar in the sand. "Voices to the voiceless."

Heavy sigh. I can feel the way the scene shifts and fades. Gets smoky around the corners as the camera pulls in tight to the embers. I take off the red and blue glasses and throw them toward the lake. I'm not sure I want to see this next part in 3D.

AR Bennett

Without the novelty specks the world is a fuzzy overlay of images with crisscrossed blue and red hues. The kids around the fire stand up and form a tighter circle. Only now they aren't in bikinis and boardshorts but the burnt orange of Erie County Juvenile Correction Center.

And they are not circled around a fire.

In the center of the ring there is a smaller boy. Scrappy is the word you're looking for. Only to be scrappy you have to scrap. This one has seen a million fights. Choreographed and stunt performed and perfectly executed high up on the silver screen. A real fight. Real fists to face and sneakers to ribs. That's nothing he's seen.

"You think you're funny?" A big chubby slab of rotten ham rolled into pimples and teeth that will never see braces asks from the center of the circle. The ring leader position. He's got the scrappy kid in a collar grip and is yelling in his face.

The scrappy one looks at me with a mix of fear and anger and sorrow in his blue eyes. "What do you call it?"

"Witty and charming." I say from the void. The scrappy kid turns his bloodied head and looks back at the big bully holding him. He smiles the smile of a boy who will tell a joke you won't understand.

"I prefer witty and charming over funny."

Punch.

Back on the ground. Busted up and beaten. It takes me a second to realize even here in the dream void, I'm rubbing the scar over my left eye habitually. That nervous touch when the chips are down. The scrappy one is trying to get up but is being pushed back down by the other kids in the circle. Acolytes to Pimple Face and his authoritarian brand of friendship.

Then out of the shadows, out of the fog of forgotten time itself, comes a folded metal chair. Wickedly swung and heavily hit. Unlike the scrappy one this is not the first hit Pimple Face has had to take. He shakes it off and spins around on the intruder. A tall and lanky older boy who stands almost a head over the others. Like someone stitched two teenagers together toes to shoulders. Wild black hair. Wild eyes.

Absolutely wild how he holds the broken bits of a Coke bottle in his hand.

"Ya gunna stick me with that?" The bully snarls. Knows he can take it. Knows a jagged broken bottle to the side can't be worse than having your hand forced onto a stove or whipped with metal coat hangers when you don't take the trash out.

Apples

And

Trees

"Maybe," the tall boy grins. "Or maybe…"

He spins the broken bottle around and holds it to his own neck. Pushes in just enough to mean business. "Maybe I'll cut from ear to ear. Blood spray like that this close? You'll be covered in it. Not a good look for you. This is what your 4th time here? Fifth? Maybe the screws come and see you standing over a corpse with blood on your big fat face and they have had enough. Haul you off to the big house. Give you the chair for what you've done. Light you up like a candle. Kentucky Fried Fuckup. Feel me?"

Jesus Christ. I can feel how dark this got even here in the void. I pull back on the 3D glasses and force the scene to change.

Scrappy and the tall boy are sitting on the bleachers away from the rest of the orange jumpsuits. The tall boy smokes a contraband cigarette. Offers one to Scrappy who smiles and takes it like it is his hundredth and not his first. "Why'd you do that?"

"Because fuck the establishment. Fuck bullies. Someone has to give a voice to the voiceless."

Scrappy laughs. He likes that. Likes the way it feels in his concussed head. Yeah…fuck the establishment. "Sounds like a punk song."

"Hey," The tall boy grins. "Maybe it is."

He gets up off the bleachers and looks down at the young scrapper coughing on his first cigarette. "Let me give you three rules to live by."

ONE: Never let them see you bleed.

TWO: You can't fight crazy.

He starts walking away. Fading into the fog of memory. "Wait what's the third rule?"

The tall boy turns back, sticks out his long tongue, and extinguishes his cigarette on it. He pops the butt in his mouth, chews, and swallows. Clears his throat with a chuckle. Both the young scrappy kid and I watch in amazement and confusion as the tall boy throws up devil horns and fades away.

Scrappy looks at me perplexed. Leaving my voice in the void to finish the Three Rules to Live By: Always have an exit strategy.

There's a crash and a triumphant cheer before I'm yanked back into the presence of Younger Me standing victoriously in the recently opened door frame of my home. Most of The Pre-Bad Bunch are hooting and hollering. Even Younger Scooby has cracked a smile.

A million odd smells come as memories that I can sense despite the busted mess of my nose. Mothballs. Dust. Lake water. Time. Wood polish and old furniture under plastic covers.

Nothing quite like the first time.

"Don't you see it?" Younger Me and Me Me say at the same time sharing a voice. Fire in our blue eyes. Righteous rebellion and rage on our tongues. "This place? It's ours."

There's a bump and a thump and I'm yanked back up into the waking. Away from the peace and back into the fray.

AR Bennett

Track Thirteen: Double Nickles On The Dime

By the time we came to a stop and my head banged against the metal quarter panels of the trunk I was blinking the cat nap out of my eyes. Nothing about the fifteen-minute drive made me feel, in any way, refreshed. At all. Whatsoever. But fifteen minutes was fifteen more than I had before I was chucked in the boot so I'll call that one a win. A draw at the very least.

The trunk lid popped open again and I had to blink out a rapidly rising sun as my eyes readjusted from the dark. The goons were ready and waiting to haul me out and once again drag my limp deadweight to our destination.

Which was exactly what I thought it'd be.

"So, it's the old trunk and dunk is it then Charlie? Your boss isn't very original. You know that my guy?"

"Why fix what isn't broken Saint?"

"I dunno. Variety? The spice of life?"

Charlie didn't respond. The goons just kept dragging me on. You'd be hard pressed to find a better spot in this whole city for some light enhanced interrogation than this old papermill. Set apart from a dwindling industrial sector that hardly anyone bothers to go to. Right on the water. Big. Empty. Secluded. Vaguely menacing already in a rusted abandoned sort of way. That unsettling feeling that places like this have where you get the feeling people should be around but aren't.

Real estate really does come down to location, location, location.

I'm dragged into the mill via large cargo doors and find myself in a wide-open space about two football fields in length. The pigeon filled holes in the roof cast strange shadows off the hulking machines left to rot in ruin in the corners. From a metal catwalk above comes the sound of sanctimonious clapping. Applause stylized satire and sarcasm.

"If it isn't the patron saint of pain in my side." A shadowy and vaguely snooty voice calls down from the catwalk. There's the sound of polished Italian loafers coming down metal stairs and within moment's I'm face to face with Barnaby Colt.

Well face to waist.

I am on my knees after all.

"I'll tell you Saint, I was surprised to find out you were at my little party. Don't you know it's maritime courtesy to ask permission to come aboard?"

"You know me. Piracy is in my blood. Gotta say you look remarkably well for a guy who's just run himself a ground."

He did look well actually. Pinstripe suit. Canary yellow tie tied in some fancy flourishing double knot. No worse for wear. Not a care in the world. At ease and comfortable. If for nothing else you had to hand it to a guy for still looking posh in a place like this. Sinking ships be damned.

"Terrible that. I had to fire my captain. He just wasn't up to the job." Colt says with mock sincerity. "Speaking of jobs, you must think you pulled a pretty nice one with the zoning council, don't you? Come to find out councilmen have expensive tastes?"

"Something like that."

"Tell me Saint. Where'd a degenerate youth such as yourself get that kind of money?"

Well, if you must know it was a downpayment from a mafia princess who will probably be cutting my balls off if I don't deliver on finding the thing that she paid me to find.

But I'm not going to tell Colt that.

"Had a rich uncle who kicked the bucket."

Colt looks over at Charlie and shakes his head sadly.

"See that's the problem with this generation Charlie, they are coddled. Had it all handed to them. My kind had to earn it. Come up with it the hard way by the sweat of our brows and dirt on our hands."

Uh huh. As if managing a collection of fleabag motels and dive bars was somehow comparable to working in the coal mines or steel plants. Here he is in a suit more expensive than the car I don't own and he is lecturing me about handouts?

"Well to be fair it wasn't my generation that covered all that natural hardwood with shag carpet, now was it?"

There's this flicker of rage in Colt's gaze. He doesn't respond to me. Not directly anyways. Instead, he looks over at Charlie.

"Charlie?"

"Yes boss?"

"Hit him."

For the second – or third? Or fourth? – in so many hours my face meets someone else's fist and my nose gives yet another sick pop. Charlie might not look like much, he looks like an accountant if I'm being honest, but he can sure pack a punch and still manages to keep that trademark Charlie smile while he delivers it.

"Anything else clever you'd like to add?" Colt asks once his goons pull me up from the chipped concrete. There's a long strand of crimson dangling out of my nose. I try to snort it out but only manage to blow a blood and snot bubble that splatters down on my shirt and shoes.

"Hmgfughhhh…"

"Didn't think so." Colt smiles. "Now you've been around the block haven't you Saint? You know what goes on here and how it goes down don't you?"

"Ughh…" *SNORT* "Yeah. They used to make paper here, didn't they?"

I look at Charlie and sort of shrug. It's a papermill after all. Or it was anyways. Charlie just shakes his head as he works some feeling back into his knuckles. Seems to have been a bit since he's had to put fist to face. This feels like organizational bloat, doesn't it? I mean why even have goons if your upper management has to do all the menial tasks themselves.

"You know Saint?" Colt chuckles humorously. He adjusts the knot on his tie so that it is just right. "You're not as charming as everyone says you are. Here's how this is going to work. I'm going to have Charlie put you in the drink, get all familiar with whatever industrial runoff has sludged up there, and then I'm going to enjoy a coffee."

There's a reason this plant is abandoned. And it's not from the lack of paper demand due to the rise of email. This plant was notoriously bad at containing their waste and in fact felt very strongly that the Great Lake the plant stood on was exactly the sort of spot where it would be a good idea to dump it.

Even to this day who even knew what biological horrors had grown around these shores. The EPA shudders to think.

One of the goons hands Colt a coffee in a Styrofoam cup and he blows thin trails of steam off the top before taking a sip. He looks down at me and smirks.

AR Bennett

"While you're down there, I want you to think long and hard about where you might have last seen a certain tape."

SMASH CUT TO:

Charlie and the goons in their mod squad suits stand in the dark and dingy interior of Brandon Lake's last known resting place. They are doing a good job of tossing the place despite it having already been tossed.

Charlie has this sour expression as if his mouth is full of ripe lemons and he uses a pocket square to cover his nose. I don't blame him. I was there too only later on when everything had even more time to settle in.

The goons pull aside the picture of the Kennedys and hey wouldn't you know it there's a safe there.

Who would have thought?

Charlie and the goons shrug the same stupid little shrug the Ivans shrugged some time earlier. One of the goons tries the nob and twists it a few times before trying the handle. No dice. Charlie shakes his head and motions for the goons to follow him out.

They duck under yellow caution tape that at this point isn't really even hanging on, where the goons get back into a big black Rolls Royce. Charlie hands an envelope to a couple of plain clothes cops – you know the type – who smile the smiles of someone being paid twice for the same job. Charlie pats the tall one on the shoulder and makes his way into the passenger seat of the Rolls.

*****

"Jesus Tap Dancing Christmas it's like a fucking clown car of criminals around here. Y'all didn't think to bring a crowbar?"

I can just hear one of the goons mumble "Told you we needed a crowbar" before Charlie lights me up with another right hook that sends stars streaking through my eyes. I used Tweety Birds as an analogy last time I took a heavy right cross right? It's all starting to blur together.

The goons look to Charlie who looks to Colt who gives the nod and next thing you know I got two thugs in JCPenney clearance sale suits dragging me to a hole in the floor that leads directly to the putrid waters below. It's not exactly glowing green but it definitely isn't Fiji Water either.

Dasani maybe.

I'd like to say I was talking my way out of this most recent predicament, that I was using my considerable charm and wit and silver tongue to wiggle free, but if I'm going to be honest here all that was coming out of my mouth was

"No."

"Stop."

"Wait."

"Hang on."

And the like. As far as comprehensive and well-articulated arguments go this wasn't.

There's just enough time for a gulp of air to hurriedly fill my lungs before I'm head first in the drink and the next sounds out of my mouth are

"Gurgle."

"Guuurgle."

"Hmgggluuugggllle."

"Murgle."

"Gurgle…"

GASP

That tasted like hot tuna left on a tin roof and licorice. I do my best to heave in air not contaminated by years of industrial toxins stagnating but I'm only mostly successful. Mostly. If I can make it out of here, I'm next in line at the local Urgent Care to get an update on some shots as soon as possible.

I'm coughing and sputtering which causes the seaweed in my hair to sway back and forth and slap me in the face with a wet thick *thwack*. I'm not sure if my nose is still bleeding profusely, or if my body is doing its best to purge mutated fish guts out of my nostrils.

"Anything you'd like to say Mr. Saint?" Colt asks in his assistant principal sort of way. Patronizing. Punitive. Rapidly losing patience.

"Ugh…umm…yeah. I never took you as a fan of punk music? Thinking of starting a band? Colty Dog and The Charlie Boys? The world could always use a new boy band. Give the Backstreet Boys a run for their money yeah?"

There's disappointment written all over Colt's face. Barely held contempt. Oddly parental disapproval. He motions Charlie to motion the goons to…

You get the idea.

"Hang on!"

Charlie raises his eyebrow. The goons stop and have that unsure look of a couple dogs unsure how to perform a trick. Colt sips his coffee casually before giving the motion for me to continue.

"If you don't like Colty Dog and The Charlie Boys how about Real Homewreckers of Erie P…"

I'm back in the water before I can finish. Something slimy and scaly slithers up my shorts and caresses parts of my me I'd rather not have caressed. Hell, I haven't been touched like that since Prom Night. It might look like I am spasming and flopping around like a pathetic fish out of water but that's because I'm spasming and flopping around like a pathetic fish out of water.

I'd like to file a strongly worded complaint to the Better Business Bureau.

It goes something like this:

Gurgle,

Gurgle gurgle gulp gurgle. Gurgle gurgle, gurgle guuuurgle gurg. Gurgleee gurrrrrrg grrrgllll. Gurgle gurgle. Gurgle.

Gurgle

Gurgle

Gurgle

Gurgle

GASP

The screen returns from 16:9 ratio to 4:3. I blink out the black bars of widescreen as my vision starts to come back from the brink of blacking out. My lungs burn. I'm coughing and spitting up puddles of foul water. My hands have started to shake in the goons grasp behind my back.

"No no no. Charlie, do it properly."

Charlie looks over at his boss with a questioning look plastered on his normally implacable face. "Boss?" He asks.

"Mr. Saint grew up on the lake. He's a natural swimmer. Aren't you Saint?"

I shake my head and wet strands of seaweed spry about. Colt does his best to not get any on his expensive shoes.

"Now you're just being modest. We've all seen the pictures. Silver medal in Districts. 100-meter freestyle, was it? Made the back page of the Tribune, didn't it?"

"Well…cough…second place is the first…cough…loser."

The man has done his homework. I guess that is to be expected when you're dealing with a small-town titan of industry. Truth be told, I've always been a bit of a swimmer. Grew up on and in the water. But my silver medal days were fifteen hundred and sixty-three beers ago. Which seems like a long time; however, I do own an illegal bar…so maybe not the best point of reference going but you get the idea.

"Where's the tape?"

"There is no way Brandon Fucking Lake ever created anything this good."

"On that we agree."

Of course we do. This is the guy who lobbied to have rock music banned from the free concert series in the park downtown. Said he corrupted the youth. Something something something about the decay of societal norms and ingrained values this country used to live by.

So why the beat down?

Why the enhanced interrogation tactics?

"Then what the fuck?" I sputter. "If it's not about the music then what's it about?"

Colt snarls. Full on rabid dog snarl. Veneers bared. Thick vein pulsing on his wrinkled forehead. With a quickness that is unexpected coming from a guy his age he yanks Charlie's gun from his holster and starts waving it about sporadically. Leaving me to twitch and dodge away from whichever direction the barrel is pointing. Also, sporadically.

I'm not the only one.

Charlie and the goons are also doing the "avoid the barrel" dance with one of the goons – the squirrely one – going as far as actually hitting the deck coming down to join me on the concrete floor.

Colt is blood red and huffing. As he yells diatribes and slurs spittle flies from his lips.

Literally frothing at the mouth. In all our nefarious dealings I've never seen Colt lose his cool. Not once has the façade of polished and put together business tycoon ever cracked.

So far, I've skated by on jokes and wit. That's long gone.

Now it's just a growing and hyper realized fear.

Genuine fear.

For my life.

I can't make out everything Colt is rambling, but the snippets I do catch speak to someone who is very close to the edge. It also doesn't get me any further to seeing the scope of the shit storm I've stumbled in.

Not at first anyways.

"You think because you paid off a councilman – MY COUNCILMAN – that that earns you a seat at the adult table? You fucking peasant. You haven't earned anything. Nothing." Then the slide of Charlie's Glock slides back with an ominous clack. The safety is disengaged. "There is nothing you think you own that I can't take away. Not your little hovel. Not your Canadian connections. Not even the fucking sand in your pathetic filthy pockets."

Now what does my Canadian connections have to do with any of this? Thought we were talking about albums?

This doesn't feel like the best time to be asking for clarification. What with a gun being pointed squarely and firmly at my head by a raving business tycoon turned lunatic. Still, there's a part of me that wants to dive into that particular part of his diatribe deeper. Before I can ask however, Charlie clears his throat and steps up to his boss. He puts his hand very gently on Colt's shoulder. All Rock-A-Bye Baby When the Wind Blows in his mannerism and on his accountant by way of gangster face.

"Boss? Maybe put the gun down?" Charlie is trying to de-escalate things. This isn't how they normally operate. Sure, they are bad, but there's bad and then there is bad. There's beating the piss out of a guy and giving him the old Trunk and Dunk then there's putting one in his head. Different levels.

There's that, yes.

But and let's be honest here, I wouldn't be the first body this lot has disappeared around these shores. This is a very convenient place to do such things. Bodies come up drown in the lake all the time. The difference being that cleaning up after a gunshot wound - or GSW if you watch the cop shows - requires an awful lot of work and that just sounds like too much hard labor. If hard labor was what this bunch wanted, they wouldn't be in this life now would they? Money for nothing and chicks for free.

Colt's manic eyes scan about seemingly taking it all in. His gray hair has come free of whatever shoe polish he uses to hold it in place adding to the overall out-of-control appearance. Doc Brown on crystal. He looks down at the pistol gripped in his hands as if it is the first time he's seen it there.

A deep breath.

A hand taming a wild mane of gray hair.

A safety snapping back on.

"Sorry about that." Colt says finally with a smile. He chuckles and flips the gun over to grab it by the barrel so that he can hand Charlie back his piece butt first. "Lot on my mind these days. Deals in the works and we all know the devil is in the details. This shit?" He waves the gun around wildly to indicate our present situation. The abandoned papermill, the sludge water, his lackeys, me dripping wet and dog panting on the floor. All of it. "Is not my highest priority."

"Of course, Boss." Charlie nods.

Colt nods. The goons nod. There's this moment of kumbaya. Peace and harmony. My heart rate dips a bit down from heart attack range. The tension in my shoulders and neck releases.

Colt nods again.

Then with a sudden renewed sense of rage and fury he SLAMS the butt of the pistol across my forehead.

A pistol whip from anyone, even someone who looks like your great Uncle Harold and has liver spots on his arms and hands, is going to fucking hurt. And it's going to leave a fucking mark.

I can practically hear my scalp ripping open.

There's this slow-motion feeling. I'm watching myself fall to the ground at a fraction of time. Beside and through me a hundred scenes from a hundred movies collide together in some fun house infinity mirror collage. Fighters falling in slowmo. Heroes and villains. Fighters and those they fought. Blood spraying from my broken nose and the new gash on my forehead. Face set in a pained grimace.

The hit knocks the ringing from my ears and replaces it with some cosmic jukebox. A soundtrack overlayed on top of reality. The machine whirs as it cycles through the album. There's a click clack as the vinyl is selected and put onto the player.

That first scratchy sound of feedback as the needle touches.

Then it's

> Hello Darkness
>
> My Old Friend
>
> I've Come To Speak To You Again

Around me there are the muffled sounds of people arguing. Shouted words. Bad noise. Above me through the hole in the ceiling the sky fills up with thousands of bats all screaming and dive bombing the former paper plant. Still in slow motion I blink as blood pours down my eyes and I can tell why the bats are fleeing. Giant manatees are chasing them. We're in the middle of a fucking sky zoo and someone must have been giving booze to these creatures.

Time comes back to normal full speed so suddenly the record seems to scratch and skip.

I hit the ground hard and just stay there.

I'm not quitting.

I'm fine.

This is fine.

I'm just…just…gathering my strength. Taking a short siesta. Recuperating. I've never been pistol whipped before. It's a new experience for me. Just take a bit to process how I feel about it. Which is not great.

The blood from my head forms a river on the concrete and as the line of red flows I start to see shapes emerge. A huge gaudy hotel where a quirky beach house used to sit. Crimson caricatures of socialites sipping Bloody Marys' between tennis matches held on red clay courts. Cigar smoke and scotch. Fancy suits. Fancy cars. Laughing the practiced laugh of high society as they look down on all the lessers. My blood forms that too.

Us.

The have nots.

Down in the red hued shadow of the hotel fighting for scraps. Turning on each other to survive. Rats in the trash.

Then I'm yanked up and the river of blood snaps back to splatters on concrete. I'm pulled up by my shoulders and propped up against the grips of two goons trying desperately to steady me and keep me from falling back over. Colt takes a very deep breath, in through his nose and out through his mouth, and smooths his suit correct.

"Earlier today," he says once he has composed himself. "I had my boys go through the little peasant shack you and your cabal of proletarian youths call home. Know what they found?"

"A…*cough*…sense…of…*cough**hack*…enlightenment?"

"Hardly." He continues. Has something on his chest he needs to get off. "No, besides the filth of your generation they didn't find anything. Nothing. Nada. No tape. No album or whatever you people call it these days. Why is that I wonder? If you're sooooo goddamn good, soooo clever and capable and connected, why'd my men find nothing?"

Because it wasn't there.

Obviously.

But I'm well past getting the sense that isn't something Barnaby Colt wants to hear.

"Okay…okay. You win. I'll tell you where it is. Just…just…don't hit me again. Fair?"

Colt nods. Please continue. The floor is yours. I look between him and Charlie. Trying to put together who's more dangerous. Charlie at least still has some semblance of calm. Struggling to keep it up. But it's there. Barely.

"Jesus Charlie. You thinking of invading Poland? Setting up a quaint bed and breakfast with complementary gas showers, are you?" I turn my attention back to Colt. Defeat stained on my face with the blood from multiple wounds. It looks like I've given up the ghost. Second place is the first loser. Bowed down and beaten. "Here it is. Here's the truth…"

Pause for dramatic effect.

AR Bennett

"We're waiting."

Get the audience bought in. Hanging on the edge of their seats.

"See I had the tape," I say slowly. "Had it on me. Then I took your mom to a nice seafood dinner and I must have left it at her house. Probably on the nightstand next to the bed."

Deliver the punchline.

Ha.

Classic.

Got 'em.

Colt's had enough. Out of patience and mercy ran dry. His rage boils over. I guess that wasn't the answer he was looking for. Of course not. I just couldn't help myself. Never gone half in a day in my life. Though it does feel like I might have poked the bear a bit.

The real estate tycoon grabs a plank of wood from a pile of industrial scrap and comes in swinging. I have enough time to push off the goons and curl into a ball on the floor before the first savage blow can connect. His aim is off, but that doesn't mean he doesn't score a hit. Pain blossoms from my thigh as the skin instantly starts to welt up.

"OKAY! OKAY OKAY!"

    Fuck

    Okay

"I don't have it. Never did. It wasn't in the safe or on the boat. But I know who does."

"No more fucking jokes. Tell me who the fuck has it or so help me Christ I'll bludgeon you to death right fucking here."

"No jokes. Fuck. Jesus. Shit." I pant. Curled in a ball. Head thumping. Leg throbbing. "Tommy has it."

"Tommy Twelve Toes?" Charlie asks. Colt's bloodlust is cooling down to a low simmer. He looks at Charlie with a confused expression.

"The one and the same."

"Tommy is underground." Charlie says. "No one knows where he is."

"I know where he is."

"Then," Colt snarls, seeing realization and recognition dawn on Charlie's face. "You'll take us to this Tommy."

"That's not going to work."

Once I'm sure there are no more blows forthcoming, I push myself up to a sitting position. Groaning and moaning as I go. Isn't that how I got into this mess in the first place? Groaning and moaning.

Different groans.

Different moans.

Colt rolls his eyes. He grips the plank in a white-knuckle clutch and looms over me. When he speaks it's through gritted teeth. Clenched so tight I can practically hear the sound of fake morals cracking under the pressure.

"And why is that?"

Yeah Saint, why is that?

"Just to be clear as Charlie pointed out no one knows where Tommy is," Stalling for time. Letting the train of thought arrive in the station. "Except for me. So, if you kill me with that bat, or in the drink, or put a bullet in my head then your best lead on whatever the fuck this tape is to you goes deep six with me."

"You don't need your legs to tell me where he is. I can shatter every bone in your body except maybe your jaw and you can still talk."

Fair point.

AR Bennett

He sure does know the 'Art of the Deal' doesn't he.

"Sure, you could do that, but I'm a liar. Are you going to trust a liar to be honest? Honestly think about it. And as to why I can't roll up with you it's because no one knows where Tommy is. Now why do you think that is? I'll tell you why. Tommy Twelve Toes knows ten languages. He knows every local custom. Even a scent of a tail or flashing lights and he'll blend in, disappear. He'll be down in Mexico with a wife and two kids sipping cervezas before that Rolls of yours stops rolling."

Now it's Charlie's turn to roll his eyes. And why shouldn't he, I'm laying it on pretty thick. I know it. Charlie knows it. The goons might suspect it, but after the recent show of sudden aggression from their master they might be having a hard time processing anything at the moment.

The only person who's not in the know is Colt.

He lowers the plank and leans on it as a golfer leans on a club. With a heavy sigh he asks me what it is I'm proposing.

"I go in – alone – and go drag him out. Once he is above ground and off the lamb you and yours can go to town on him. Give him the whole Gitmo Treatment."

"And I'm supposed to believe that you'd do that? Give up a friend? Just like that?"

"Well, we're not exactly friends."

Maybe more friend of a friend.

Maybe not even that.

Colt thinks it over. He kicks it around in his head. There is this pungent pause as we all wait on bated breaths. He kicks up the plank like Gene Kelly kicks up an umbrella and leans it on his shoulder. "How do I know you won't just rabbit yourself?"

"Where am I going to go man?" I laugh. "There's nowhere where I can run that you couldn't find me." Flattery might go a long way here. It's not like I'm lying. The earth isn't big enough if Colt sets his mind to it. It's his world. We just live in it. "Put a tail on me if you have to, but keep it discreet."

Charlie looks over at his boss who shrugs. Colt kneels down in front of me so that his face fills my vision. His breath smells like five decades of Cuban cigars and Russian Caviar.

"Okay," he says with a wicked grin playing across his wrinkled face. "Here's what you're going to do. You're going to find this Tommy…what is it Charlie?"

"Twelve Toes Boss."

"Why?"

Charlie and I exchange glances. It's not that hard.

"Uhh..because he has twelve toes Boss."

"Fucking kids these days." Colt sighs. "Fine. You're going to find this Tommy Twelve Toes and you're going to bring him to me. If you even think of running, get a clever idea up in that thick skull of yours you'll be the patron saint of being buried in shallow graves. Clear?"

"Crystal."

The big bad boss man waves his hand and the goons once again get their mitts on me, hoisting me up and off the ground. Behind me I can hear Colt tell his troops to drop me off back at the beach house, but before they do, put something down in the trunk.

No need to stain the leather.

As I'm being hauled off, I can't help but feel a type of way about what just went down. As in…

AR Bennett
What

The

AR Bennett

FUCK?

Track Fourteen: Damaged

The trunk comes open and yet again there's Charlie standing over me taking up all the sun. Only this time he offers a hand down to me and helps pull me out.

"What the hell was that, Charlie?" I ask as soon as my feet touch sand.

"Sorry Saint." He says and I think he means it. "Tensions are high right now."

"Why? Why are tensions high right now?" Everything hurts. I feel like I'm owed more than a few answers. "We didn't come up together Charlie, but we come from the same place. At least tell me what in shit's name is going on? Give me that."

We did come from the same place. Same story, just different chapters. His chapter is a few - well maybe more than a few- before mine. Charlie is Charlie because he's clever with accounting. Creative with numbers. More than that Charlie knows how to keep books and throw left hooks. Helps that he is dog loyal by nature. Makes him into a great Number Two.

But right now…

Who's he loyal to?

And what's all this got to do with Brandon's phantom tape? Or me and my lot for that matter. I know Colt has a hard on for the KBH, that's old news. We've been doing that song and dance for a while now. This feels much more urgent. Much more hectic and head off unscrewed. Colt's always been a smooth operator, you don't get where he got without some moves. He has made it so he personally doesn't have to get his hands down in the muck. Has people for that doesn't he? So, what's he doing flashing gats and swinging planks into the thighs and sides of guys like me. Colt has people for that. He's his own boss.

Isn't he?

Charlie chews on his bottom lip. His leather loafers shuffle on the sand. Now I know Charlie knows that whole spiel about Tommy and ten languages, about blending in and disappearing, was just a load of bull. But he did me a solid back there and didn't say anything when he easily could have.

We came from the same place after all.

"It's a bad deal Saint." He says finally. "You know what happens when two opposing weathers collide? Cold air over warm water?"

I do know what happens.

I've seen it many, many, times in my life.

Bad storms. Thunder snows. Rough weather.

Lake Effect.

"What's that got to do with me Charlie?"

"We're all in deep water now Saint." Charlie shrugs. "Let's just say someone is pulling strings that haven't been pulled in a while."

"Your boss doesn't strike me as the type to heel to a leash."

Hands up slightly in defense. Slight unsure chin nod. Another shrug. "Know what they say Saint? It's not the size of the dog."

It's the size of the fight.

I shrug. What are you going to do?

What am I going to do? No seriously. What's a guy to do? I'm asking. Any recommendations would be useful, because so far, I've managed to get myself beat up not once but twice. Been in a boat crash. Had guns pointed at me. Punched, kicked, slapped, nearly drowned. I'm a bloody and beaten mess barely keeping it together. Everyone and anyone who is anyone, all the staples of this world of ours from the suits to the soviets, all want a piece of this action.

Then there's me.

Born on the outs.

"Trust me Saint," Charlie says as he moves to get back into the air-conditioned comfort of the Rolls Royce. "I'm not happy about how this shook out either. But I've got strings too. So, be that as it may, if you don't deliver Twelve Toes? If you run? If you pull off some Bad Bunch scheme? It's going to be me who puts a bullet in the back of your head and I'll do it too."

I've already turned away from the trunk and have started making my way to the beach house. I give a thumbs up over my shoulder.

"Ain't no strings on me Charlie."

"Keep telling yourself that Saint."

What's a guy to do?

I enter my beloved speakeasy and it takes about eleven seconds for me to see the place is absolutely trashed. Colt wasn't kidding when he said he'd sent his boys to give the place a once over. Scooby is sipping a coffee while sweeping up the place. Scooby likes to have things neat and orderly.

Always has.

Always will.

"You look like you could use a coffee." He says as I stumble in.

For those of us up all night coffee and donuts held little to no appeal. I walk past him leaving a trail of drips and drops as I go. From behind the bar, I grab a bottle of Corona, pause, think it through then proceed to grab another. I pop the top of the first one off the counter. Someone had dumped the limes on the floor – probably the squirrely goon he looks the type – so with a wince of pain I bend down and bring up a slice. There're dust bunnies and whatever else stuck to it.

Whatever.

Into the longneck it goes and I chug down half the beer in a big, prolonged, gulp. Dust bunnies and all.

"Watson still underground?" I ask as soon as the beer is empty and after cracking open another one.

"Yeah," Scoob says as he sets the broom aside and approaches the bar. "Got out of there when things got hairy. What would her father think and all."

Yeah, what would the captain of the organized crime task force think?

I don't blame her. To be honest I was wishing I had gotten out of there before I had too. Scooby is giving me the once over. Concern spread across his dark face.

"Did Nikki do that?"

I shake my head and sip my beer. Nope. She did not. Though I do truly believe given the opportunity she would relish the chance. Even if it was just witnessing it. The gash on my head burns. My busted beak throbs. My leg and ribs and wrists and

Just

All

Of

It.

Hurts. Everything hurts. I've had some nights well wasted in my time but this one was taking the cake. And the cherry. And the ice cream too. Best not to dwell on it. Gotta keep moving. I have to keep my mind on task. Can't stop here. This is bat country.

"The Boys have any luck?"

Now it's Scooby's turn to shake his head. Didn't really expect otherwise but there was that little sliver of hope holding out. Hope that Benny Bones and Alaska and Handsome Black would have turned up something. Anything.

"They've hit the streets hard man. But everyone is either hiding or too high to help. You know Brando's type. He never was one for the quality of the company he kept."

I wonder if I'm in that group.

I'm perched on the bar and sipping my beer through aching lips. I can't taste it properly because I can't smell it properly so it just comes off as lukewarm fizz. Gingerly I touch the pistol whip gash on my head. It's deep. Deep and angry. At least some of the bleeding has stopped. A bit.

"Get us a med-kit, would you Scoob?"

"If not Nik, want to tell me what happened?" He asks over his shoulder as he rummages around for a travel sized med-kit.

It's just the two of us. Everyone else is either hitting the street or underground away from the fray and out of harm's way. Just us and the Kelso Beach House. I study the walls and the ceiling. I'm trying to commit each imperfection, every crack and chip of paint, to memory. Could be the last time I truly get to appreciate the place.

"Colt happened." I say finally. I've already opened another beer. This feels like a three-beer type of morning.

Scooby is fiddling with our meager supplies of Band-Aids and gauze. He looks again at the gash and selects a few butterfly bandages with a "I guess that's what we got" type of shrug. The cut needs stitches. I know that. Scooby knows that.

AR Bennett

Some butterfly bandages and super glue was going to have to be enough. No time for a visit to the clinic. No time for proper stitches.

"I didn't think brutality was his business."

Normally Scoob would be right. Business was Colt's business. Something since last night and this morning had the old dog learning new tricks. The trunk ride back from the papermill had given me some time to myself and some time to think. It wasn't all there but pieces of the puzzle were fitting together.

"This is going to sting." Scoob squeezes the super glue against my head and yep, he's right. It stings all the way from my head down to my soaked sneakers. He pinches it together and places a few butterflies over it. "This have something to do with a mysterious envelope of cash that you managed to give to a certain councilman?"

"No. Yes. I dunno. Maybe." I say. "The tape actually."

"That tape? Brando's tape?"

"The one and the same."

Scooby stands back and scratches his beard. He's clearly confused. Hell, so am I. Are you?

Even for Scoob this is a lot. He's got more skin in the game than he lets on. More meat on the bone other than just keeping court with me. If I fill the books with bad ledgers, he is the one who keeps track. Keeps a calculator and knows the numbers. Likes to have things in order. Neat. Everything has a spot and everything in its spot. If we were to ever franchise our little batch of Libertalia I'd be the CEO sure, but Scooby would hold a corner office and a plaque reading CFO.

One usually follows the other.

"What's Colt Industries got to do with a punk record?" He asks finally. His dark eyes searching mine for meaning, concern tugging at the corners of his mouth.

Record.

As In:

Recording.

Huh. Haven't thought about it like that. What's a record if not a recording. The collected sessions of an artist at work. Doesn't mean the artist has to be a musician. What was it John Lennon said? "I'm an artist man. Give me a tuba and I'll get something out of it." Something like that. Not a big Beatles guy personally.

What if the artist at work had a different type of instrument? Pliers and fingernails perhaps? Hammers and bones. Jumper cables and nipples. Give an artist a tuba and he'll get something out of it.

I get off the bar and retrieve the last of Brandon's Columbian Bam Bam. There's less than a zero chance this nose candy is going to actually go up my nose. Not in this state. But a lightbulb has gone off and I can feel the movie montage brewing as an explanation comes top of mind. For that, and for what comes next, I'm going to need all the giddy up and go I can get.

I pour the remaining powder into my mouth and fucking chew it.

Yeah. We're at that point.

"You've got that look." Scooby says as the beach house around him starts to fade. Pupils dilate. Chemical induced clarity comes into focus.

"You still have those papers?"

"Of course." He goes to the wall and opens a secret chamber behind some wood paneling. We run an illegal speakeasy. We've gotten pretty good at squirreling things away when the times call for it. Plus, he did say he would keep them safe.

Scooby is a man of his word.

He lays the file out on the bar and uses a few half-drunk beer bottles to hold the crumpled and warped pages down. Somewhere far overhead the cosmic soundtracks quietly picks up. The steady growing riff.

"Okay." I say as the riff builds and builds.

(There's a good chance I'm not actually hearing some well composed and fitting cinema style soundtrack but instead I'm just suffering from a concussion. A brain cloud maybe.)

Okay.

So here it goes. This could be the up-all-night running scared. It could be the coke. It could be the beating. Brushes with death. Brain bruises. But

Holy shit.

I see it now.

Fucking bear with me. We're going for a ride.

"Right. We know that Colt has a Viagra hard on for this area, yeah?"

Scooby nods. He looks around as the beach house becomes more and more hyper stylized. Like the set of some late-night crime show. "Is this what a series of Smash Cuts feels like?"

"Oh shit? You feel it too?"

"Uhh…"

"Never mind that. Just stay with me. Colt wants this place bad. Wants to tear down the Goon Docks. Build himself a new Club Med. Casinos and cigars and fancy cars. Wrought iron fences to keep the personas non grata out."

"But Goonies never say die."

"Now you're getting it. You can't tear down what you don't own. And we're not selling. What's a villain gonna do?"

"Umm..."

"Yep. Exactly. I knew you'd understand. If he can't get around us, he's going to go through us. Get it? What does all this look like to you? Plans right. Blueprints. Building schematics. Club Barnaby Colt."

I'm jabbing my finger at the folder. It could be the coke but it does sure look like that sort of thing. Maybe if you tilt your head.

"We can't sell because, one we don't want to, but two because we don't own it."

"Then who does?"

"Lake Effect Entertainment LLC."

"Why does Brandon Lake own our bar?"

Good question.

SMASH CUT TO:

There's me and Brandon Lake sitting on his yacht. The rest of the band is preoccupied by some hookers splashing about in the water. This was a few years ago. You can tell because Brando looks like Brando and not some burnt out junky version of himself.

"You know the old abandoned beach house on Kelso?"

That's me if you can't tell. Gotta keep up. Gotta be quick with me, I'm from Erie PA.

"I want to buy it."

Turn it into a bar. Build it up. Make it mine. A home for The Bad Bunch.

I get up from the deck chair and address the camera directly.

AR Bennett

It's not a bad idea. There's not a lot of job offers for someone with my past. Having a "legitimate" business would be good for just that. Business. The only hiccup is that because of my record I can't go through the normal channels. Plus, that and I'm about as liquid as concrete at the moment. Strapped for cash as it were. If we are going to cut some red tape and get around those pesky legalities we're going to need some serious scratch.

Rockstar scratch.

Certified platinum.

"Goddamnit!" Brandon yells and throws his beer in the lake. "I'm in."

Deadly.

I wink at the camera and it's

SMASH CUT TO:

Brandon Lake, Tommy Twelve Toes, and I all standing in ill-fitting suits in some office downtown. A very nice lady who looks like a Barb or Debbie or perhaps just like your Aunt Susan sits behind a cluttered desk full of cat pictures and slides us a stack of papers. I can see Alaska and Benny Bone's handiwork all over it.

"Sign here." Your Aunt Susan says.

And we do.

The ink's not even dry before it's

SMASH CUT TO:

Me and The Bad Bunch standing on the big wrap around porch of the Kelso Beach House. We raise cold Coronas up and clink our glasses together.

Off in the distance, wrapped in shadows, a sleek black antique car rolls to a stop. The window rolls down and you can see Colt staring daggers our way. In his liver spotted hands is the crumbled plans for some Colt vision. The next big thing. It's quickly and angrily being ripped to shreds. His wrinkled face is flush with anger. A lot of money has gone into whatever the future is and Colt wants to make sure his future stays bright. Didn't expect a fast ball from the freeloading fast and loose up starts. Never would have seen a clever con coming from us. As the tires kick up sand and the black car peels away you can see the wheels turning in Colt's gray head.

There's other ways to skin a Saint.

"Cat. There are other ways to skin a cat. You crucify or burn saints." Scooby asks as the 4th wall starts to crack and crumble around the edges.

"Your mom must be so proud that catholic education is coming in handy huh?"

He rolls his eyes and shakes his head. Has this habit of putting his hands on his hips when he wants to make a point stick. "Not sure if it's the night you've had, the coke, or some combination of both but I'm just trying to make sure you stay on track. It's getting pretty muddled as it is without you making up your own proverbs."

"Okay if you say so." I bounce from one foot to the other. Left right left right right left left right. Teeth grinding. Pupils dilated to eleven. "Can I continue?"

We're back in the now though the Kelso Beach House is still buzzing with that ultra glossy HD film quality.

"Did that actually happen? Colt was here when we moved in and I just missed it?"

"Best not to think about it. Just try to keep up."

Scooby does his best to get his head back in the game. I'm practically ping ponging off the walls. Working up steam. Building momentum. That steady building riff gets louder and louder as we push forward full speed ahead.

Damn the torpedoes.

"What's all that got to do with Brandon's album though?"

The million-dollar question.

"What if it's not an album? What if it's a recording?"

"I don't see what you mean? What's the difference?"

Glad you asked Scooby. I'll show you.

SMASH CUT TO:

Colt and Boris 'The Butcher' Mikhailov standing on a verdant and sunny golf course. They are a number of Singapore Slings in and Colt is getting animated. He's pink in the cheeks and loud in tone.

What does he care? Not like anyone will hear him. He own's the fucking club.

He's going on and on about this cherry piece of property and his bright vision for a better future for it. The Butcher nods his head. He's clearer. More focused. What are a few Singapore Slings going to a guy who has been raised on Russian vodka straight from the tit? His smile is genuine. You can tell he means it. Still animalistic though. Not like they call him Boris 'The Bubbly' or whatever.

"Da. I'm in. I'll put my best man on it." Boris offers his hand and Colt eagerly shakes it. The Butcher smiles. Colt smiles. Only The Butcher holds his smile for a bit longer than is normal. There is no mistaking the predatory glint and glimmer in his cold dark eyes. "We are in this together, yes? But Barnaby…May I call you Barnaby…if it goes sideways that's no good. There will be consequences, yes? And you…my drook…friend yes?...will have to answer to me."

Colt smiles the smile of a man holding the paw of a tiger or the fin of a Great White. He nods. Good. Good. Yes. Yes. Business is business. When Boris finally let's go of his hand and Colt can feel blood pump back into his knuckles, he turns from his new partner in crime and gulps the gulp of a man who might have just made deals with The Devil.

I can see the lightbulb start to flick on in Scooby's head. He taps the stack of papers with a bony knuckle. Under a smudged beer ring on a signature line in black ink for the world to see is an initial. Not BC

But

        BM

"Ah." He says. "And Boris the Butcher's best man is actually not a man at all."

"Nope. Apples don't fall far from trees."

"And then you two?"

"Had drinks, yeah."

Scooby rolls his dark eyes. "Riiiight. Just drinks."

He snaps his fingers and it is

SMASH CUT TO:

Me falling back onto a bed with sweat soaking my brow and the sheets. Porcelain fingers come into frame from off camera and caress down my chest. I turn my head and look directly at the camera.

"Any particular reason we're here or are you just feeling a bit pervy?"

"Just proving a point." Scrooby shrugs. But he does sneak a quick peek at the shadowed figure straddling me.

And who wouldn't? What red blooded American wouldn't sneak a peek at a former ballerina stretched out acrobatically and bare. Perked up and puffy. Light sheen of sweat on porcelain skin.

I shake my head and snap my fingers.

Scooby shakes his head as the world comes back into focus. He's looking down at his recently snapped finger with a sense of awe and amazement.

"That was incredibly satisfying."

"Tell me about it."

Low whistles and catcalls. Hubba hubba. Cartoon wolves with their jaws on the floor.

He gives me one of those looks that says he was talking about cosmically cinematic abilities and not my time rolling around in the sheets. Then that look fades and is replaced with another one of concern and maybe morbid curiosity.

"Wait, did you catch feelings?"

"What? No."

He holds up his fingers threateningly. Inches apart. Just about to snap. I scowl and hold up my half-closed fist vaguely threateningly. Give him that "I mean business look." He holds his ground. We've done this song and dance before. Old hat. Felix and Oscar.

Finally, he caves and puts his fingers down. "Fine. It was just the once?"

"Yep."

"Really?"

"You and I can do this all day Scoob, but maybe we could get back on track here before everything goes off the rails entirely?"

Square jaw nods up and down sending wavy brown hair bouncing. "Fine. But we're not done with that."

"Square deal. Remind me when we're not in the shit yeah?"

We're ripping now. Well past the point of no return and deep into it. That riff has built up into a wall of sound that is covering the world in a blanket of growing noise. The drop is coming. Can you feel it? Getting close to

Something

Not sure what

The drugs are clouding things. Speeding it up too much. Take a breath and get back on track.

Right.

Where were we? Oh yea...

"Daddy Mikhailov puts his precious little princess in charge. It's not like they haven't done this sort of thing before."

SMASH CUT TO:

Alisa Mikhailov in her red bottom high heels and posh gangster chic. She stands on the neck of some book worm looking guy as he shakily signs off on some very legal looking documents. The Ivans are having a field day tearing the place apart behind her. Papers and personal belongings are thrown this way and that.

She looks up from the whimpering little man and addresses the camera.

"We have done this before."

SMASH CUT TO:

Alisa Mikhailov and her Ivans stand shoulder to shoulder with Colt and his Charlie Boys and they all look down at a bloodied and beaten Brandon Lake hog tied in dog chains and weights.

AR Bennett

They are all on Brandon's boat in the middle of the lake. Not another soul around. Just blue waters and not much else. Colt holds out a thick stack of papers and demands for Brandon to sign them.

What's a guy to do?

Bloodied. Beaten. Bound and gagged.

One sympathizes.

He puts his mark on the papers with sadness welling up in his bloodshot eyes. Hoping against hope that they'll now let him go. Sorry man. It's not going to work that way. Loose lips sink ships and all that.

Gold Tooth Ivan kicks the rockstar square in the chest and sends him backwards off the deck of his boat and into the drink. The chains and the weights do their part and down down down goes Brandon Lake.

Except he's a sly fox still.

As he hits the bottom of the lake kicking up muck and scaring a school of fish the gag comes off. Bubbles come out of his mouth as he tells the camera

"I am a sly fox still. Got 'em in the end, didn't I?"

Scooby is now fully committed. He's nodding along as the puzzle pieces spill out of my mouth and start to form a clear picture on the bar.

"The tape."

"Yep. The tape. Or recording. Album. Whatever. Brando recorded the whole thing. Used his floating studio turned crack house to get all the beating, all the threats, all the everything on tape. Their whole blood confession rendered in Dolby Digital for the world to hear."

"How'd he get it off the boat?"

"What?" my heart is just fucking racing. Sweat is building on my brow. You think I got time to be filling in plot holes right now? Holy shit. This is my brain on drugs.

"The Tape." Scooby repeats slowly. There is a growing concern as blood from my broken nose starts to leak onto the file. He calmly slides the folder away from the splash zone. "If he's at the bottom of the lake how'd he get the tape off his boat and away from the bad guys?"

"Huh."

"Yeah. Huh."

Synapses firing at the speed of sound. Hearing colors and seeing shockwaves of sonic booms. Right. Right right. Right rightrightrightright. Think Saint. It's so close you can taste it. No seriously you can taste it. Why do your ideas taste like Pepperoni Balls? Because I'm from Erie PA that's why. If you've never had a pepperoni balls its pepperoni

Obviously

Wrapped in dough and then fried to a golden perfection.

What the fuck are we doing here? Right. Plot hole. The tape. Fix that. Got to fix that. I'm fine this is fine we're all fine no big deal no need to come off the rails just think it through keep thinking it through you got this we got this we got…

"Are you okay?"

"Uhhh…I don't know. It's in my thumbs. I can't feel my liver."

OH!

DUH!

"Tommy took it." There it is all neatly wrapped up. I think? Maybe? Can't really tell. Not focusing so good.

"Twelve Toes?"

Are we going to do this bit again? Where someone states Tommy's last name and I say one

AR Bennett

and the same? No. Fuck it. I think we've had enough. I just nod my head. Up down up down up down up down

Down.

Down I-79

Down south.

But north of Pittsburgh.

"I need your car."

Track Fifteen: Zen Arcade

I've never personally experienced a cocaine induced breakdown, but I'm going to go out on a limb and suggest that might have just been it.

It took some convincing but Scooby ultimately hands me the keys to his car. His beloved car. We all have our kinks and the great golden beast is his.

"I dunno Saint, it's fairly flimsy at best."

"Yeah. No. I know. The flamsiest. But the more you sink your teeth into it the more it starts to sound like fried gold. We got the Mikhailovs here on our shores. Colt doing his Colt thing. Brando intertwined somehow. Follow the strings my guy. This web makes sense from where I'm standing."

"Does it though?"

"Who gives a shit? If it makes sense or not? They want the tape, they expect me to get the tape, and they will kill anything that gets in the way if I don't."

Scooby nods. He is still apprehensive. I don't blame him. I'm apprehensive too. This whole thing has gone sideways somehow and I'm beginning to feel that no matter how this shit storm got started, I'm going to be the one left holding the bag. Last one left without a chair when the music stops.

He's had me chug down nearly a jug of water and shoved some food in my face. I'm still absolutely fucking buzzing, but it is more of a background tingle. The mania of the previous moment has subsided. A bit.

"You sure you don't want me to come with you?"

I know that he is asking for two reasons. One, he wants to watch my back. We're partners; one usually follows the other. And two, he wants to ensure his car, his pride and joy, doesn't end up upside down in a ditch. I don't blame him. I wouldn't trust me either.

"I'm sure. This is something I gotta do on my own ya know?"

He throws me the keys underhand and I snag them out of the air. The still morning air is already starting to heat up as the sun climbs ever higher in the sky. It's going to be another hot one, and time is running out. Still, I'm not rushing off just yet. I'm dragging my feet. I stand there and fidget with his keys for a moment. Head down studying the sand. Thoughts still in overdrive.

"You think they are still going to be mad?"

"The Twins?"

I nod my head slowly. It's not like I don't already know the answer. I'm just hoping my best friend will tell me otherwise.

"I love you Saint, you know I do, but you are you." He says with a laugh. "They are definitely still going to be mad. Have you ever thought maybe it's time to settle down bro?"

Now it's my turn to laugh.

"Yeah. That's tomorrow's problem."

"There's always tomorrow."

"Unless there isn't."

He doesn't say anything to that. Neither do I. I just get into his car and fire it up. The big beefy V8 engine fires on the first turn. Well maintained and well cared for. Scooby to a T. I let the engine idle for a moment enjoying the rumble from the Detroit muscle.

This is feeling like a goodbye.

I roll down the window and lean out.

"I'll be back. And if I'm not then well…you know what to do."

"I don't actually." Scooby says with a sad smile. "There's no Kelso Beach House without the patron saint of the Bad Bunch."

"Okay well just don't cry at my funeral. Gives people the wrong idea about us."

Scooby laughs. His dark features brighten for the briefest of moments. I want to tell him to take care of young Benny Bones, take care of Alaska and the rest, take care of the KBH. I want to tell him to go on and FSU if I don't come back. Fuck Shit Up. There's a lot I want to tell my oldest and closest friend. My right-hand man.

But I don't.

This isn't a fucking goodbye.

I just throw some devil horns his way out the window and put the golden muscle car into gear. Point the hood south. Spray some sand his way when I pop the clutch and spin tire in a manner I know that he hates. Then he and my Kelso Beach House are fading into the rearview.

And we're on the road.

There is something that is pure Americana about driving a vintage car down an empty stretch of highway with the sun at your back and hard-hitting punk music coming from the speakers. The sense that the Founding Fathers would have been doing the exact same thing if given the chance. With the right type of eyes, you can see the Red, White, and Blue flapping juxtaposed over the azure sky above.

Felt good.

Edinboro is not that far from Erie. About an hour. But that was an hour more of peace than I had in the past 24 so far. I let the sounds of 'Lake Effect in Affect' wash over me. Brandon Lake's voice from beyond the grave. A ghost that endured.

Isn't that what we all want?

AR Bennett

To have something that is ours. That endures. That will last the relentless march of time and stand as a reminder that we were here.

We were fucking here man.

In this place. In this time. Against all odds.

As the wheels under me spin on black asphalt the wheels in my head turn as well. An hour to myself. To think. To put it all together.

That's how all this started didn't it? Back before the Tape. Back before Colt and the Soviet Sally. Back before boat crashes and blow and dark clouds, bad times, hard weather. Behind me the uneven and cracked highway of I-79 stretches out into the past until it arrives at that moment that started it all.

I wanted something that was mine.

The Twins wanted something that was theirs too.

The Skittles Twins.

Understanding why we call them the Skittles Twins requires a tad more nonlinear thinking. They aren't as easy as Tommy and his two extra digits, or Alaska and his size or Scooby and his uncanny resemblance to a cartoon dog owner. This one requiring bit more mental gymnastics even more than me. I'm holy. Full of holes. That's easy enough.

The Skittles Twins are the Skittles Twins not because they remind people of Skittles but because they are M&Ms.

Micah and Mary.

M

And

M

Brightly colored candies. Like I said, mental gymnastics. Sometimes things aren't wrapped up in a neat bow.

And they run the puff game in these parts.

Well, they did. Until I fucked it up.

A younger version of me is sitting in the backseat. He's fresh faced and full of passion and pride and drive to come up in this world and leave his mark. He slides black wayfarer sunglasses down his working nose and raises an eyebrow at me in the rear-view mirror. As if to say "Go ahead. Tell them."

The Twins and I have history.

The kind you've no doubt come to expect from me and the other kind also.

Younger Me just shakes his head and goes back to staring out of the window as the scenery passes. I keep my eyes on the road ahead. I'm looking forward, focusing on the road ahead, looking to the future because behind me is always cloudy except for when I look into these past one-night stands.

Younger Me snaps his gaze away from the window and fits me with an angry stare. Okay it was more than a one-night stand. Much more. He nods before returning his stare back out to the countryside that threatens to engulf the road on each side of the car.

I keep the hood of Scooby's great golden machine pointed south. Edinboro is south of Erie and north of Pittsburgh. Situated in the middle of nowhere and sandwiched between some farms.

A college town – Home to the Fighting Scots – and not much else. It's the perfect place to set up an illegal grow operation. Out of sight. Out of mind. Built in clientele in the dorms nearby. It's no wonder that the ganja game sprouted here.

It's said that crime is often connected. This is true. We all have our ears to each other's grapevines and our fingers in each other's pies. Not how that came across. Get your mind out of the gutter. We don't have our fingers in those kinds of pies…

AR Bennett

...though...

You could make a very convincing argument about me.

Not here nor there. Younger Me in the backseat chuckles silently.

Crime is connected, but it is also compartmentalized. The same people that run 24/7 speakeasies on the beach and deal in goods of questionable origin are not usually the same people that grow and distribute green. If you want to party all night on duty free Mexican cervezas imported from Canada you come to Kelso Beach. If you want a smoke and a toke you come to Edinboro.

More specifically you come to the Copper Coin.

You come to the queens of super skunk Sheba. The green thumb goddesses.

You come to The Twins.

Out here, away from the beat cops on the street and the tycoons in their towers and the hands that snag and drag you into the underworld of the city, you can be anything you want to be. Who's looking? The cows?

Like me, Micah wanted something that was hers. Unlike me she had noble intentions. At least at first. See Micah is one of the true few that come up the very hard way. Harder than the streets. Her rise wasn't against external factors and forces but internal ones. Her war was fought on the inside.

Micah had been sick.

The type of sick that is stacked against you to claw back from. Vegas odds.

But claw back she did. With some dedication, help from her numero uno right hand girl, and a bit of grass. The toke helped her heal. Which is why she wanted to give it back to the people. Holistic. Helping. Herbal.

Like I said, noble intentions.

Then there was me.

It's like Charlie had said: You know what happens when two conflicting energies collide?

Storms start forming.

There is a burst of static from the radio followed by the repeated high pitch tone of the emergency broadcast system coming through the speakers. A robotic voice starts talking in a prepared message. Younger me silently says the words coming from the speakers in unison. This is a message we are all familiar with to the point of having it memorized.

THE NATIONAL WEATHER SERVICE HAS ISSUED A LAKE EFFECT STORM WARNING FOR THE FOLLOWING COUNTIES:

ERIE || SUMMIT || WATERFORD || LE BOEUF || EDINBORO

Above me the sky is cloudless and blue. The static laced emergency broadcast message fades away back into the past where it belongs and is replaced with hard hitting metal as if the music had never left.

Micah wanted to help people. I want to help people too, but my help usually comes as a side effect of me helping myself. Micah and I have a vastly different idea of the meaning of 'The Tide Rises All Ships'.

And there is opportunity in the grass game.

A big growing market.

Profits a plenty.

My Canadian contacts across the border were curious. Mexico doesn't have a monopoly on the cartel game. In a move that was more Colt than Saint I put The Twins in contact, brokered a deal as it were. Something to benefit everyone.

AR Bennett

Only the whole thing blew up in my face and whatever history The Twins and I shared was not enough to shade me from the fallout.

Fucking Canadians.

Known worldwide as generally rude and unsavory characters. They certainly earned that reputation I would say. Younger me in the backseat sighs silently and shakes his head slowly. I get his meaning. Can't blame the Canadians.

Micah and Mary certainly don't.

They blame me.

As they should.

I'm not sure who I am more worried about out of the two. But I'll burn that bridge when I get to it.

*****

I pull Scooby's muscle car into the gravel parking lot of the Copper Coin. To my surprise the place is packed, too packed for eleven in the morning. The big steel bodied car can barely fit between rows and rows of an assortment of bikes. Choppers and bobbers. Hogs and Fatboys. Panheads and Sportsters.

The bar was alive and awash in a sea of black leather chaps and bad attitudes.

Certainly a different customer base than I remembered the chill Cheech & Chong crowd drawing in.

As I get out of the car a big guy covered in 1% tattoos and bound in black leather swaggers over to me with intent in his hard eyes.

"Hey!" He growls. "Angels only pal."

Just ignore the man with 'Born to Kill' inked on his knuckles. Ignore the sounds of a hundred roaring and revving engines. As a person who has flirted with the edge, the drug game and the good times of a life well wasted, I am familiar with having certain events unfold in front of me. Younger versions of myself sitting in the backseat. My dead grandmother crawling up my leg with a knife in her teeth. An almost cinematic stylized control over my own narrative. I can take a lot.

But this trip? No one should have to endure this trip.

At least not if they had the day I've had.

So just keep walking.

The big biker puts his palm out and presses against my chest pushing me back. I've made it through this night without throwing a blow. On the defensive not the offensive. So far, I've kept my cool and calm. Taken my beatings and not reciprocated in kind.

But if there is one thing that I hate.

Hate. Hate. Hate.

Loathe entirely.

A gesture that can send me over the edge. One thing that sets fire to my blood and puts me in get some mode.

That's being poked in the chest.

I can feel the cosmic jukebox start up hot and heavy death metal building behind my ears.

"I said," the bike emphasizes each word with a poke and a push. "Angels only. Fuck off."

"Angels huh? How about Saints?"

This confuses him. Throws him off guard. That metal music builds and builds. I'm having a hard time seeing my surroundings through all this red. In his confusion I seize an opportunity. Grabbing his wrist as he goes to poke my chest again, I wrench it around while simultaneously kicking a knee to bring the big guy down a peg.

I have to say. It's a fucking cool move. All kung fu and Jackie Chan. It could be the night I've had, could be the cocaine, could be the creeping sense of catastrophe, but right now with the big biker dude down on his knees his wrist cranked in whichever direction I want under my control.

I feel like a golden god.

The feeling fades. Quickly. Because by the time I look up I'm surrounded by a circle of bikers in black leather and each one of them is pointing a gun to my head. To the man. Not a single knife. Just Glocks and 1911s and Smith and Wessons.

It seems I've brought Krav Maga to a gunfight.

Everything is very still. Except for a bit of tumbleweed in the parking lot which looks very much like it would like the wind to blow it about thematically. But the wind is busy messing about with some wheat fields down the road so the tumbleweed just shrugs sadly and sits there.

"It's ok boys." A smoky voice comes from the bar. "You can let him go."

The group seems unsure but ultimately decide to heed the instructions. They lower their guns and back up just a fraction of an inch. Lower not holster. Not put away entirely. This still has the potential to turn into a turkey shoot at the drop of a hat.

"You too Saint. Let him go."

I let the biker go and he slowly rises to his feet. As a sign of good faith, I put my hands up. Palms to the sky.

"Now you all know the rules," Micah says casually as she descends the stairs. She moves with a cat-like grace that seems to cut through the tension. "We will not tolerate violence at our establishment."

To emphasize this there is the distinctive clunk chunk of a pump shotgun being pumped. Which is odd considering she isn't holding a pump shotgun. She isn't holding anything in fact.

Mary is.

Bloody Mary. Coming from the shadows behind Micah. Literal backup.

"Gentlemen, this is the patron saint of the same old same old. And despite what this incident might otherwise tell you, he is actually capable of playing nice and can on occasion be a good guy." Micah moves to further help the big biker up. She seems genuinely concerned. "Knuckles, are you hurt?"

"Only my pride ma'am."

I smile. The worst kind of hurt. There is a good chance that me and this Knuckles will have unfinished business. Wounded pride is a wound that festers easily. Turns to rot quickly. Hard to forget.

Knuckles knows this too and he stares daggers toward me. From the pocket of her tight jeans Micah pulls out a small bag of leaf. She gently presses it into Knuckle's big hand.

"On the house." She says, "for the trouble."

"Thank you, ma'am."

"Saint if you'd like to follow us?"

You can tell the Twins apart because one is tall and slim with wavy dark hair while the other is shorter with her shortness accented by curves. One is unarmed and the other is holding a shotgun. One is even tempered while the other is hot headed.

You can tell The Twins apart because they look nothing alike.

I nod to Knuckles. The up down head tilt of respect. And follow The Twins inside. The Copper Coin is best described as a bar. You know the type. You've probably been in your fair share exactly like it. It has a bar and barstools and booths. There are posters about beer on the wall.

It's a bar.

A dive.

AR Bennett

A hole in the wall in the middle of nowhere.

There's no need to spend a ton of ink on this. You can see it in your mind's eye. Just close your eyes and picture a place that smells like college kids for $.25 draft Wednesdays and Bike Night Fridays.

It looks like a bar.

But it isn't a bar.

Not like how my bar isn't a bar. Not like how the Crooked Eye is more a concert venue than a bar. The Copper Coin is not a bar. It's a front. A very good front. Hidden in plain sight. Right under the noses of anyone who would come sniffing about.

"Locals are a bit rougher than I remember."

It takes a moment for my eyes to adjust from the bright sunshine to the dim dark of the bar that's not a bar's interior. Micah leads our little group with Mary and her twelve-gauge scattergun of fun bringing up the rear. Leaving me, yet again, between a rock and a hard place.

"Times change." Micah says over her shoulder.

"That they do."

"Do you?"

That is probably left to be seen if I'm being honest. I haven't figured that part out yet. There's been a lot going on in a short time. Who can say if with everything going on I've experienced some meaningful form of character development. A proper arch. Hero's journey.

But I'm leaning towards no.

No, I have not.

Same old. Same old. Same Saint, different day.

"What brings you down the 79 Saint?" Mary asks from behind me. The way she's holding that shotgun indicates this is a question not of the rhetorical variety.

Oh, you know. Tapes. Torture. Mistakes and the mafia.

Those old chestnuts.

Not that I'm going to tell her that. I'm on thin enough ice as it is. Yet again bringing trouble to their doorstep. Darkening their days with my trials and tribulations. My own unique and uniquely personal brand of chaos. As far as legacies go the signature Saint style is hard to beat.

"Figured I'd go to Kinzua State Park. Rent a cabin in the woods. Find a nice quiet spot and make some smores. Have a glass of red and stare at the stars when they show up."

"That sounds nice," Micah says. "Peaceful. You could use some peace Saint."

No, I could use a tape. A record. A

Whatever.

I could use Tommy Fucking Twelve Toes and whatever secrets he is keeping in his junk addled head. Peace isn't even on the menu. Not even in the same ballpark for what I need. Not the same state.

"Peace would be nice for sure." I lie. "I could use some company? You know a couple of beautiful ladies who might like to join me?"

There's the increasingly familiar feeling of a hard metal being pressed against my head. Good thing I'm thick skulled. Otherwise with the regularity of how many barrels have been put towards my brain I would have started to worry.

"What no Canadians available tonight?"

Point well taken.

The problem had not been me introducing The Twins to my Canadian contacts, though that in of itself was a bit of a faux pa, but it was what the Canadians had done once they were connected. Rapid expansion. Forced growth. The Twins had founded the grass game out here to get away from the rules and regulations that govern our little underworld. When they tried to explain that, tried to course correct the ship I'd set sail, the Canucks responded with decisive and effective force.

"Easy Mare Bear. I think Saint wouldn't have come all this way just to dig up old histories. Isn't that right Saint?" Micah calms. I nod.

"He's not to be trusted Micah. He's the pretender."

"Hmm. Maybe you're right. His energy does feel off." Micah stops walking and looks me over. "Still, this is a place of calm and contemplation is it not?" She motions her partner to lower her weapon.

Mary lowers the shotgun with a grumble. I rub the back of my head where the barrel had been. For a place of calm and contemplation there sure seems to be a lot of violent tendencies going on. A whole lot of guns for a sanctuary to self-healing and energy adjustment.

"Calm and contemplation? I'm to take it that the Hell's Angels out front are what? Emotional support hooligans?"

"You of all people know what it's like to make hard compromises for something you love, Saint. The Angels are here because we need them to be. Because they are the best way that we can keep what's ours, *ours*."

I can't fault her logic. This whole hell-bent night has been in service towards keeping what's mine, *mine*. Maybe my vibe is harshing up the mellow. There's no denying that I'm spun up and strung out. Ran all night. Running scared. Bouncing from one problem to another without even the slightest chance to slow down.

I could stand to enhance my calm.

Breath in. Breath out. Open the door and step backwards into your cave. Find your power animal and just slide.

Nah.

"Look, you're both right. I'm obviously not here to go to some cabin in the woods. Nor am I here to revisit history."

Hands tapping on my thigh. Impatient twitches like ticking clocks or time bombs. Slight shakes from the giddy up going through my legs and down to my toes.

"Then why are you here?" Micah asks, watching me intently. Behind me Mary cradles the shotgun in her arms and watches me as well.

You can tell The Twins apart because one is calm and the other is a wild card shuffled into a loose deck. You can tell them apart because they are nothing alike.

"I'm here to find Tommy Twelve Toes."

"And what is it you need with Thomas?"

To beat seven shades of shit out of him until he tells me what I need to know, tells me where this tape is or even what it is so I can get out from under this mess. Save the Kelso Beach House. Save my life. Have a beer I can actually taste that isn't tainted by the blood of my broken nose. If I need to hang the rat fucker up by his toenails to get those things then that is what I need from Tommy.

Don't let the drugs and booze and the sleepless night do the talking. Breath in calm.

"We need to have a chat."

"Just a chat?"

Micah is nearly as tall as I am. We can look eye to eye fairly easily. Though it's hard to tell what her eyes are searching for in mine. After a moment I nod my head.

"Just a chat."

Mary comes from behind me and stands next to her partner. She's still got the gun. Still considering using it, if for nothing else than old time sakes.

"This wouldn't have to do with why the streets in your neck of the woods are alive with pain would it Saint? The reason all the dark ponies up that way on the lake are running scared?" Mary asks.

"It's all that and a bag of chips."

"Let me get this straight, you've yet again managed to bring destruction to our door."

"I just need to talk to Tommy. Tie up loose ends. Sort through some things. Get our energies back in alignment. Isn't that what this place is about?"

Just a talk. Nothing more. Just a friendly chat between old acquaintances. A friendly calm chat that if I have to, I will pull out his fingernails with a pair of pliers and use soda to waterboard the ever-loving fuck out of him.

I'm keeping my options open.

But no sense in telling The Twins that. No reason to harsh their mellow. Any further. Then I already have. Again.

"You always had a silver tongue, Saint." Micah says finally and with a soft smile. I nod my agreement and for her to continue. "Thomas came to us a broken man. Haunted by the death he feels he caused."

"Uh huh." The puff game never killed anyone sure, not from the smoke itself, but Tommy's a junkie's junky all the way down. Rotten through. I don't see the green giving him a 180. It seems the growers have gotten a bit too high on their own garden. Peace and love through puff. Healing harmony guarded by Hell's Angels.

Give me a break.

"Is he around then? Tommy? Or is he rearranging his heart chakra somewhere else?"

The Twins talk among themselves leaving me to tap a Lake Effect in Affect song on my thigh. The early afternoon sun comes in from the window and sends prisms dancing around crystal chimes and dream catchers. It would be rather pretty if it wasn't for the ticking clock hanging in those rising rays.

The sun rises ever higher.

Time is running out.

"Okay," Micah says finally. "We'll take you to him. On one condition, you tread carefully. Thomas is in a fragile state."

I put my hand to my heart and assure them that I will be Mother Theresa. Unless I won't be. Unless it goes the other way. But I don't say that part. Keep that card close to the chest and tight to the vest.

Micah moves behind the bar and motions me to follow. She uses a set of keys to open a door to a small back office. At the back, behind a neat and organized desk, there's another door. This one too requires a key to open. When it opens instead of shelves for bar supplies and glassware there's a set of stairs that seem to go down down down for a long time into the deep. Micah takes a step down the stairs and I step after her. Mary brings up the rear.

Rabbits in white waistcoats.

And just like Alice what is at the bottom of the hole is so far and removed from what was up top that the change can only be described as fantastical. A strange new world.

Welcome to Wonderland.

The room at the bottom of the stairs is a room in the sense that warehouses and aircraft hangars are technically rooms. It goes on and on for yards not feet like a football field hidden underground.

AR Bennett

Everything is lit in the rave scene purple of blacklights that bring all the bacteria and fish guts I've almost forgotten about on my shirt to life in radioactive neon greens.

If the size and scale of the space and the blacklights weren't enough the real awe inducing scene was seeing that the entire space, from wall to wall and corner to corner, was packed with row after row of pots and each pot holds a sprouting plant that reaches up toward the ceiling.

Super Skunk Sheba.
The Devil's Lettuce.
Whacky Tobaccy.
Ganja.
Green.
Marijuana.

There's enough here to keep both Cheech, Chong, and Willy Nelson in the hip happening grooving mood for many years to come. You could have ten Woodstocks down here. Twenty maybe. It seems The Twins hadn't come out worse for wear with the Canadians after all.

If anything, their operation has seemed to have gotten bigger.

No one is giving me a medal for that. Where's my warm welcome?

Smack dab in the middle of this mecca of Mary Jane, this hidden oasis of herb, standing hunched over by a plant is one rat faced fucker alleged sex offender ex junky black bag manager of promising punk bands and personal confidant of Erie's First Son

Tommy Twelve Toes.
Fucking finally.

"Saint?" Micah asks quietly, her long fingers touching my elbow softly and preventing me from charging down the aisle between the plants and grabbing Tommy by the collar. She has a sadness in her eyes that I can't shake. Despite all my rage that sadness seems to urge me to keep a level head. "Just a talk."

I nod my head.

"Just a talk."

Her fingers linger for a second on my elbow. Skin on skin. The soft touch of two people with histories. I could have smiled, offered some charm or appreciation of her touch. I could have done a lot of things. Every gesture could have been a new chapter heading in the right direction of a story unfinished.

Oh Micah. I wish I could have put the tears back in your eyes. I pull my arm away slowly and turn back to the real reason I am here. Every canvas that I paint is a masterpiece of my own mistakes. Micah nods sadly. She pulls her hand back and places it on her hip as protective a gesture as Mary cradling her shotgun.

Walking down between the plants gives me time to study Tommy. He's smaller than I remember. Deflated. As if the wind has gone from his sails. He is also not as rat-like. Sure, he still has the pointed nose and large front teeth, those haven't changed, but at this moment he doesn't look like the world has forced him to claw and gnaw his way into or out of something. His once greasy hair is now washed and fluffy.

As I get closer, I can hear him humming a slow sad song that takes me only a few steps to place as one of Brando's tracks from back in the band's Emo phase. You know the type even if you don't know the tune. We all had our Emo phases. Some never left.

Tommy looks up from pruning a bush of bush and for a very brief second – a blink and you'll have missed it moment – there's that old rat-like flight or fight that flashes over his face when he sees me standing there. In that nanosecond his eyes go feral and wild again just as I remembered them and just like that he's back in the race. Back in the maze. Then it's gone. Replaced with this sanitized Zen like calm.

Sure.

We're all capable of change. It's just

A smoker's smoker when the chips are down.

He keeps humming his sad song and keeps pruning the green leaves. After running all night I'm not sure this sense of calm coming from him and trying to take hold in me is a new state of mind, finding clarity in the chaos, or just a contact high. There's this sense I've gotten somewhere. Found something. But whatever it is, it is still cloudy. Like trying to hold smoke in your fists. He snips one last branch before turning to look at me properly.

"The heir apparent. Have you come to kill me, Saint?"

"Why would I have come to kill you, Tommy?"

Tommy shrugs. He fidgets with the pruning scissors for a moment before going back to trim another plant. Finding peace in repetitive motions. Something to do with his hands that isn't holding and lighting a crack pipe.

"It feels like the end of the world out there. Knew you'd survive. Even if you had to make deals with devils. Maybe killing me is the price they asked you to pay?"

The thought had crossed my mind. How far was I willing to go? To keep everything? On the drive down here there was the moment, that brief moment, where I considered crossing that line and becoming a real bad one.

But then I'd be them and not me.

"Thought hadn't crossed my mind, Tommy."

He nods and keeps humming. This time a different tune from an earlier album. I know this one too. He pauses long enough to look up at me again with these sad wounded creature eyes. "That's a shame Saint."

"Why's that Tom?"

"Because in the end I always sort of hoped it would be someone I knew. Feels like it would make the transition easier."

"You knew lots of people Tommy."

He stops pruning and laughs the laugh of a man who's watched his soul drain down the hole in the needle and come out the other side. It's the chuckle of someone who has seen the better days being in the rearview mirror and knows that no future is ever guaranteed.

"What a crowd we keep in this little world of ours huh? The Twins told me there was quite a turn out at the funeral. I…I couldn't bring myself to go ya know? Couldn't do it. Felt if I went it would make it all so real maybe? Does that make sense, Saint?"

It was your gear that put Brandon down this path Tom. Don't make me lie to you. Say you couldn't go to watch an empty coffin get lowered into the ground because you weren't the one who put it there.

"Tommy, Brandon had a tape in the end. Something important. Something that I need to find."

"I loved that man Saint. He was class. A real rockstar. Brandon Lake had it all, the money, the cars and boats, the sex game not even you could beat no matter how hard you would inevitably try. Had it all. Didn't care for any of it. Not a single bit of it. Only the music mattered to him. That's how you know he was a genuine rocker. Only the music is what meant the most to him."

Is he…is he tearing up? Is that what this is? The sad sad ballads of lost souls who've escaped the junky boneyards. Somewhere far overhead the cosmic soundtrack picks up. It's faint. Just that initial ringing in my ears that is melodramatic and softly growing.

"Tommy, did Brandon send you a tape? It's important."

Tommy Twelve Toes nods his head up and down and up and down. You can tell he isn't here in this moment anymore. He is somewhere else where the memories don't hurt so bad and the scars aren't so fresh.

"I see a lot of him in you Saint." Tommy says sadly. Too sad.

What the fuck is this?

"You and him share a lot even after going your separate ways. You're both the last two great survivors. Born on the outs. You two versus the world. If someone could win, if someone could beat back the wolves, it'd be one of you two."

"I've given it all up ya know?" He continues. "The junk. The life. Except for the bush. But a joint won't hurt, will it Saint? A bit of grass to keep the thoughts calm. Other than that, I've locked the gear away in a smoke proof coffin and nailed it shut. Brandon…I know what you thought of him towards the end…but he's a good boy. Underneath it all."

"Tommy what the fuck are you getting at?"

"I'm sorry Saint."

"Why Tommy?"

He turns and faces me fully for the first time. There is the red of super skunk Sheba in his eyes, sure, but then there is the red of sorrow and regret and sadness too. The soundtrack builds. Blood begins to pound behind my ears.

"Brandon had me pick up a great number of things."

This is your captain speaking.

"Boxes of unfinished songs and notes."

Please put your tray tables in the upright position.

"There were all sorts of albums and private things. His yacht was just chalk full of memorabilia and bits of this and that. Things that if made public could make a great big payday."

Fasten your seatbelts.

"Tommy what did you do?"

"I didn't…I didn't have anything left, you see? I'd been run out. Down on my luck. Then when this studio in Santa Monica came knocking. Came with briefcases of cash. I didn't see another way out. Thought I'd do my boy one last solid as his manager and manage things for him. Thought he'd have liked that."

Tommy Twelve Toes, former manager of Lake Effect in Affect and personal confidant of missing, presumed dead, lead singer Brandon Lake, picks his gaze up from off the floor and fixes me with a sad stare that speaks in definitive tones.

"What did you do?"

"I sold it. Sold the lot. It's all gone."

We've just lost cabin pressure.

The world around me spins on a strange axis. The plants feel far away and claustrophobic all at the same time. The breath catches in my chest and I feel hot blood pump first to flush my face then up into my eyes as I start to see red. Tommy is still explaining what he did and why he did it but I can't hear him over the growing pounding in my ears. I wouldn't believe it even if I could hear him properly.

There's the initial gut punch that this little rat fuck has turned this time's last punk icon into a sellout – handed over his legacy to some corporate sound machine that will tune it up and crank it out and make Brandon Lake into some autotuned pop star to make a buck. There's that feeling and then underneath that there is the realization that all of this…this fucking night

The beating

The drive

The blow and the beer and the barging in on old histories

Has

Been

For

NOTHING.

No.

I refuse to believe that.

"Bullshit."

I'm speaking through clenched teeth. Low and dangerous. The words come out as peace and calm get further and further in the rearview and the steady beat of white-hot anger pushes up to the surface. The music is growing louder.

"Bullshit. He wouldn't have let you do that. He would have stopped you."

"He's gone."

I hit him. Hard. I don't know if I meant to. But I did. The blood is pumping in my ears and there is rage on my tongue. If I don't really know where the first hit came from, I definitely know where the second and third ones did. Tommy is cowering at my feet, holding his hands up against the rain of blows. Micah is yelling. Mary is yelling.

I'm yelling.

"HE FUCKING TRUSTED YOU! YOU ALWAYS DID HIM WRONG. DID WHAT YOU DID FOR YOU NOT FOR HIM."

I'm not mad. I'm furious. And I'm not sure if it's about tapes or interrogations or threats. We're past that. This is about someone taking advantage of my friend. Of someone I looked up to. This is about putting trust in places that it doesn't belong and and *and*

It's about a lot of things.

Tommy is whimpering and sniveling sure, but there is a readiness in his eyes. There is a this-is-it set in his bloodied lip. The bell has been wrung and the bill comes due. I can feel the pruning scissors in my hand. The cold metal is just there in my touch.

Younger Me stands silently in the rows of plants and watches with morbid curiosity as I lift Tommy up by the nape of his neck and press the sharp points of the scissors to his chest. Behind the apparition of the past Mary has her gun drawn and is charging my way. There are a great many images playing through my head as the music builds to a fevered pitch. Packed concerts and houses on Kelso Beach. Beer pong and best friends. Mistakes and memories.

All I need to do is push. Apply a bit of pressure.

I'll be cut down before the first drips of Tommy's blood drops on the floor.

Younger Me just sort of nods. It's not like we knew we were going to die in our sleep. At least it will come from someone I know. A friend. Once. At least there is that. Tommy takes a raspy bloodied breath and nods. He puts his hand on mine and helps guide the scissors to where his heart would be. His eyes tell me we can cross this line together.

The edge.

AR Bennett

That line that separates those who have seen it from those that haven't. The difference between being a bad one in a Bad Bunch and being a Bad One. A real bad one. One who has gone over.

Tommy nods.

I snarl and scream and rage. Spit flies out of my mouth and blood bubbles form in my busted nose. The vein in my forehead pulses fresh hot blood between butterfly bandages and super glue.

It would all be so fucking easy.

Just a press.

A twist.

A loud blast and then a fade to black.

Easy.

Simple.

Doable.

Not me. The pruning scissors drop from my hands and clatter on the concrete floor. I let go of Tommy's neck and step back. Hands up. Heavy breath coming hot and hard out of my lungs. Tommy doesn't look happy or relieved or satisfied. He just looks sad. Sad that whatever happens next is still going to be on him, that he's still got to go on carrying the weight he carries and living with the regrets he's created.

"Congratulations Tommy. You're the baddest of a bad bunch. You killed Brando with your black bag of tricks, your junk and your gear, and now you've killed us all too."

"I know."

Fuck. No tape. No nothing. There's a good chance there never was. Or maybe there was and I just bet on the wrong direction. Who knows. Doesn't seem to matter in the end. The cards were stacked against me from the start. The house always wins.

There's a polite cough from back by the stairs. Knuckles is standing there looking a bit confused about the situation playing out in front of him. Micah goes to him and engages in a hushed conversation. Mary is still keeping me in her sights.

When they are finished talking, Knuckles walks back upstairs. Micah comes over to me and gently takes my hand in hers.

"There's a problem upstairs." She says softly. Her eyes flick to her partner and Mary seems to read her meaning. The silent unspoken communication of two people closely tied together. Mary lowers her gun and turns on her heel to head back upstairs.

Micah is hard to read. There are layers of emotion played out on her face. She gives my hand a little squeeze. I hope she can see my apology in my eyes. I hope she can see how sorry I am that I brought all this trouble to her doorstep.

Again.

I squeeze her hand back gently before letting go. The queen of the grass game and the patron saint of impending apocalypses.

"Would that be the wolves Saint?"

"Seems like it Tom."

"Would you mind if I tag along then?"

I nod. Sure thing Tommy. Let's go face the firing squads together. After all, we came up together. Ran in the same crowds. Both played our parts in this drama. Front row tickets to the end of the world.

Who wouldn't want that?

AR Bennett

Track Sixteen: ...And Out Comes The Wolves

We head up the stairs with me being the last in the conga line. Behind me the grow house is as quiet as a tomb. Younger Me stands there under the blacklights and watches as we move forward. By the time the secret door in the back office closes the only thing down there is the grass and the ghosts.

Outside the windows I can see a kerfuffle unfolding. The Angels are squaring off with two large, bald, ogre shaped men in garish Hawaiian shirts.

The Ivan's have picked up the scent it seems.

Micah and Mary watch as the big Russian heavies push and shove their way through the crowd of bikers. With their attention divided I take the opportunity to snatch a set of keys from the bar. I push them in my pocket before anyone can be any of the wiser.

There is the faint whisper of a plan forming in my tired mind.

I clear my throat and pull the attention back on me.

"Uh…well…this is on me. Looks like I've darkened your door yet again. Whatever happens next, I want you to know your grass game will stay out of it."

"A Red Sun rises Saint. How long do you think it will be before that blood spills from your shores to ours?"

"As long as I can."

That's the best I can do. What has been set in motion is in motion. Rome wasn't built in a day, but it did burn in one. And here I am holding the match. Deals with devils. In deep waters. Over my head.

Got a few more cards to play still though.

But before that there's history that needs addressing. Thoughts that need saying and feelings that need to be felt.

"Micah I'm…"

She laughs. Shakes her head. "Don't say you're sorry Saint. It wouldn't be like you."

I smile. When she's right she's right. Knuckles and Tommy have moved toward the door. There's the old rat coming back in Tommy's face. That old gnawing will to survive. Knuckles is gearing up for combat. I take my place next to them and put my hand on the door handle.

"Knuckles, I don't know you but I like the cut of your jib. You strike me as a guy who might be interested in cracking a few commie skulls."

"Son I was kicking commie ass before you were out of your dad's balls. Semper Fi."

Well shit. Storm the beaches and God bless all of his misguided children.

"Once more into the breach Saint?" Tommy asks.

"Sure Tommy."

AR Bennett

It's classic spaghetti western cinema. The three banditos. Holed up in the saloon. Black hat cowboys causing a raucous out in the coral. One last ride. Guns blazing. Even Micah and Mary are ready to bring the noise.

We step out into the light.

I swing the door closed fast before The Twins can make it through. From my pocket the key goes into the lock and I'm left staring at Micah's sad face in the glass. I wink before tossing the keys to Knuckles who catches them easily out of the air.

The Ivan's have seen me at this point and are now making their way forward with determination.

"This door doesn't open. They don't come out and no one other than your boys go in and then only when this thing is said and done. Clear?"

Knuckles nods. Hoorah. Maybe I can keep one promise today. Keep them out of it. Keep all my mess from falling on their heads. High above in the cloudless sky the soundtrack kicks in as the big Russians push their way through the crowd in slowmo.

Time to face the music.

"Tommy?"

"Yeah Saint?"

"This new you? That include any cardio?"

The Ivans are yelling for me to come with them. Now. Da. Da. Be right there comrades. Just a moment. The brightly colored shirts are in sharp contrast to the sea of black leather. They are not hard to miss.

I walk out to meet them in the crowd. Behind me trailing at a safe distance is Younger Me, he's watching the events unfold with mild interest. Behind him is Tommy who is watching everything with much more enthusiastic interest. Rat-like eyes scanning from one person to another, sizing them up and frantically sweating through exit strategies. I make it to the first Ivan. It's hard to tell if this is Dumb Ivan or Gold Tooth Ivan but it really doesn't matter.

"You!" Whichever Ivan This Is growls. "Give us the tape. Now."

"You know I actually just listened to it. Had ourselves a nice little jam session while you lot were driving down here. I gotta say compared to their earlier work this one sort of sucks." From the corner of my eye, I can see Younger Me smile a silent confident smile. He's very flash in his proper matador outfit. With a flourish he unfolds a red cape and stands in waiting. "Sucks a lot actually…maybe not as much as your pinko commie mother does. But we all know why her face looks like an egg now don't we?"

It takes a few stunned seconds for the insult to sink in. But when it does This Ivan lights up with rage. A pissed off Russian bear on the charge. Or bull. He's not the lightest on his feet to begin with and seeing red has made him more crazed than coordinated. He telegraphs his big haymaker and I easily step out of the way at the last second. Younger Me snaps the red cape up and Ivan crashes head long into a line of bikes, knocking them over like dominos.

There are rules in our little underworld. A big one is: Never touch a biker gang's bike.

If you ever wanted to know how to turn a parking lot of a dive bar into a proper ballroom blitz, how to kick off a right good old fashioned ultra violence riot, you could do worse than this. This is a masterclass. A clinic. A case study in flashpoint crowd behavior. Ivan pulls himself up from the tangle of handlebars and exhaust pipes and it's already too late. The bike crowd descends on him.

AR Bennett

Chaos descends with them.

All hell breaks loose and suddenly I'm in the middle of a maelstrom. Fists flying everywhere. Screamed insults hurtling through the air. Madness. Absolutely madness. And exactly what I needed.

"Tommy?"

"Yeah Saint?"

"Run."

And we do. Hard. Pushing our way through the crowd. I've got Twelve Toes yoked up by the scruff of his neck and half stumbling half dragging him along with me. It would have been nice to make it to the Great Golden Beast, but that was looking less and less feasible as the circle of black leather-bound kicks and punches and roaring Russian heavies slugging it out in every direction was tightening around us.

I narrowly avoid a roundhouse thrown by…someone. Bounce off of someone else who spins around and throws a punch which I duck and that hit has the wet hard-hitting sound of him punching someone else.

Looney Toons.

Yakety Sax.

Just chaos.

Still yanking Tommy along, I get us out of the thick of it and we push, legs burning already, across the parking lot and into the tree line surrounding the bar. There's a shot, the big loud obnoxious BOOM of a .50 cal handgun, and a chunk of tree in front of us is smashed to splinters. I glance behind and I can see it's an Ivan gripping a nickel-plated Desert Eagle and pointing it our way. He's made it out of the crowd and is resuming the chase. His partner, The Other Ivan, isn't far behind. Cracking some skulls together to open up a runway through the crowd.

I know what you're thinking. That's your big plan? Yelling run and then running? I agree. As far as well thought out, grand scale, and verbosely articulated plans go this isn't. But it's what I had available to me at the moment. I've been running all night and now I'm actually running. Legs pumping. Chest heaving. Booze and toxins sweating out of my pores.

At least the chaos with the Angels has bought us a window. Gave us a head start. I can't squander it. Just need to go head down and ears back into rabbit mode. That's the plan I came up with, that's the situation I'm dealing with, the cards I've dealt myself. Gotta make the most of it.

We run.

Say what you will about the junky, but Tommy had some rat gas left in the tank. Whatever Zen vibes he had been chasing before I arrived, whether he found that absolution he was seeking or not, had been replaced with that old gnaw and claw and fight to survive as soon as the bullets started flying. I'm basically on pure adrenaline and not much else. The giddy up is long gone. I'm dipping into my own rat reserves just to keep up with the former band manager.

Into the woods. Crashing through branches and foliage. Tripping over loose rocks and exposed roots. Worn in low-top Chuck Taylors are a great shoe for doing just about anything, stylish and cool and can be worn on a wide variety of occasions. Running full tilt through the underbrush is not one of those occasions. Every step forward I can feel a blister forming on my heel as the canvas rubs against exposed skin.

Soon enough, I'm sloshing in sticky hot blood that pools around the soles of my shoe and makes my feet slippery and unpredictable with each step.

AR Bennett

Somewhere the cosmic radio is cranked to eleven. A high tempo high energy riff is shredding the sky as we crash blindly through a tangle of green. Every time I'd risk a glance back there are the Ivans. Their breathing coming fast and hard under Hawaiian shirts. Neck muscles screaming. Pistols gripped in sweaty hands. Two big Russian Rhinos charging through the bush.

A slip

A trip

A tumble and near fall. I get my feet back up under me at the last second and keep the momentum moving forward. Looking back is not the way to go. The Ivans are there, no doubt about that, but rubbernecking is not going to keep me ahead of the game. Ahead of the reaper.

Focus eyes forward.

And just crack on.

The branches snag at my skin and add to the collection of old and faded scars with bright red new ones. My legs are screaming. Ears full of pounding and punk music. Arms swinging wildly trying to eke out just a drop more speed.

Somewhere off to my right there's a cartoon rabbit in marathon attire keeping pace. Legs spinning in big complete circles. Locomotive steam coming out of his long-pointed ears. As he frantically scrambles on, he looks over at me and shrugs as if to say "What can you do? Trix are for kids amiright?"

My toe catches a root that came out of nowhere and this time gravity turns off. One second, I'm running full tilt keeping pace with my own looney hallucinations then the next I'm ass over tea kettle flying through the forest. Coming to a stop in a pile of dry leaves and sticks. Dirt on my tongue. Mud in my ears. Vines and twigs stuffed up my shorts. The reptilian part of my brain is screaming two equally loud and equally conflicting messages.

GET UP

And

LEAVES OF THREE

While the first is not that complicated to parse out, the second is a bit of a head scratcher. As I struggle to pull myself back up and back moving forward the literal actual urge to start scratching starts.

Shit.

Leaves of three. Leave them be.

Every kid who grew up in the woods along the lake knows this rhyme. Because those that didn't spent a summer caked in calamine and covered in angry red itchy bumps and rashes.

Poison Ivy.

Well now we have that going for us. Too late to do anything about that now. Just don't focus on it. Keep running. Tommy is pulling further ahead. He's got that primal fear fuel pumping through his veins. Up ahead in front of him the summer sun streams through some trees as a clearing cuts a break through the green hell.

If I can just make it to that then maybe there is a chance. Risk a quick and frantic glance over my shoulder. One of the Ivan's is falling behind. Which Ivan?

The other one.

No. Not that one.

The other one.

Which leaves this Ivan to deal with. I need a change of strategy. There's a big tree ahead and to my right. Fallen branches. Big and thick about the size of my arm. The cartoon rabbit has skidded to a sliding stop and through the dust cloud has undergone a costume change. Gone are the runners' clothes. Now he's decked out in full baseball gear. Black and yellow stripes. A pirate logo grins on the chest.

Not a bad idea.

I gotcha bunny.

Without breaking stride, I swing behind the big tree and scoop up a thick branch on the fly. I can hear the huffing and puffing of this Ivan coming up behind me. About as stealthy as a drunken elephant on spring break. The branch feels heavy in my hands. Got some weight to it. The crashing footsteps get closer and closer until it's swing batter batter swing.

The Great Bambino

The Sultan of Swat

The crowd goes wild. It's a homerun! A homerun! A gold tooth goes flying out over the outfield catching rays of early afternoon sun as it goes. Rage. Ruin. Seeing red again. I just keep whacking until I hear either the branch or bones snap. Then keep hitting some more. Until I'm done. Then I chuck the branch turned ruined bat and make a dash for first, second, for third.

Keep running the bases.

Don't look back. Don't waste this opening.

Just keep running the fucking bases and bring this home.

As I run on, I can't help but wondering if I had finally crossed that invisible line. The barrier between being a bad one and a real bad one. That was a fucking hit if I do say so myself. I put some heat into it. Full grip it and rip it. Feet planted, hips twisting to add mass to the swing. I've spent this whole rotten night and most of this terrible morning trying my best to not stumble over that line. There's a good chance that now I already have.

Too late to look back now.

Fitting that it was a Russian who once famously said: "If he dies, he dies."

Tommy's pushed through up ahead as he crashed into the opening. A road. A road is good. I can use a road. He's slowed up enough to allow me to catch up and pull ahead even.

Look left.

Clear.

Look right.

Not clear.

The biggest baseball bat I've ever seen takes up the entirety of my vision. An actual proper baseball bat, not some branch imitation. It takes up the sky in front of me the way you'd think of gods as enormous. With perfect crystal-clear clarity, I can read each letter carved into the bat's side.

LOUISVILLE SLUGGER

When you make a bonehead horror movie mistake your life doesn't flash before your eyes. There's no time. No montage of happier moments, or sitting with girls on the beach or drinking cold ones with your buds. No rewind and going back to the beginning. There's just this big fucking bat coming at your face and behind that there's Charlie grinning his annoying Charlie grin.

You might have time to open your mouth and let out a stupefied

"Oh"

And then it is

CUT TO BLACK

AR Bennett

Track: Bonus Track

FADE IN

Interior – Day

    The Crooked Eye has never looked so bright. Or so clean. I've also never seen this place so deserted. There's no Nikki Sixxx. No mosh pits. No underage kids licking off '*X*'s on their hands. Just me, an empty bar, and an empty stage.
    Save for one man.
    A spotlight clicks on adding to the overall too brightness of the space. Soaking up every watt of it in center stage sitting on a wooden stool is Brandon Lake tuning an acoustic guitar.
    Brandon looks good. Healthy. Alive. He's in his trademark black ripped jeans and faded black Ramones t-shirt. Hair pulled back in a bun with a rubber band from his wrist. It's free of tangles and sweat knots. He doesn't look up as I slowly approach the stage. Too focused on the music.
    "I'm I dead?"
    "It's not looking good for you Saint."
    Hmm. Figures.
    He tweaks a few knobs and strums a few stings. Satisfied with the sound he plays a song I'm not familiar with. It's slow and sweet with just the right dash of sorrow and sadness thrown in for flavor. There are backend notes of rage that I can feel on my tongue as I swish the sound around and savor

THE BAD BUNCH 215

the profile. He plays on for a bit and I let him finish. When he's done, he sets the guitar aside and pulls out a Zippo from his ripped jeans, I can see the "I HEART ERIE" decal on the side. The heart has been scratched out to form an "A" in a circle.

He sparks the lighter with a flourish and lights a smoke that has materialized in his mouth. Takes a drag. Pulls the smoke into his scrawny chest and exhales it out toward the ceiling. It's spilled oil in water technicolor and carries notes from songs forgotten and unfinished.

"Why'd you do it man? Why couldn't you have stopped?"

"Could you?"

"I wouldn't have taken the entire world down with me."

He blows a few smoke rings and stares at me. Hands on the holes ripped into his knees. Maybe he's waiting for me to go on, to take the plunge and ask the questions that need asking. Or maybe he just doesn't have anything else to say. There's this long pungent pause that spans centuries. Outside the sounds of waves crashing against the sandy shores carries through the brick and mortar of the dive bar turned concert venue turned place in between places.

Finally, I take the bait.

Need to know.

Have to ask.

"What's it all mean, man?"

"Don't you know?"

Not really. I have my theories. A thinker's thinker when the chips are down. Brando nods as if he can see my thoughts written across my face. He picks up the guitar again and resumes strumming chords and riffs. It's a while before he looks up and smiles sadly.

"You were always good at putting it all together Saint. The clever one out of all of us. But you forgot the Golden Rule."

"What's that? Treat others how you want to be treated?"

He laughs. Shakes his head and laughs. I laugh with him. It's good to see him laughing again. Free from the junk and gear and wear and tear. Good to see him center stage and taking up every inch of spotlight. It's good to see him. He clicks open and shut the lighter a few times in a rhythm only he knows. One last chuckle.

"God no Saint. We treated ourselves like death, didn't we?"

"You maybe."

"You too." Click clack goes the lighter. Open shut open shut. "You're here with me after all aren't you?"

Good point. Can't argue that. For the first time I realize there are no itchy bumps bubbling up on my arms and thighs. No stinging scratches from where I'd collided through tree branches and thorn bushes. No scars of any kind. No faded cuts. No nearly perfect circular cigarette burns. No longer covered in holes.

Huh.

I try to rub off this odd light that seems to cling to my skin. A shine not from the lamps or the sun. Try to think of something else other than this light that comes from nowhere and everywhere.

"What's the Golden Rule then Brando?"

Click

Clack

Open and Close

"The Golden Rule Saint is," he says finally as he pockets the lighter and picks up the guitar again, "you can't control chaos my guy."

Then it's the sound again. Edgier. Heavier. All the old hits and staples. Certified platinum. I know this tempo. Know this sound. All the classics.

"So that's what this is then? Chaos? A collection of events unfolding and untethered with no real meaning?"

"Is that so hard to believe? That's all any of this is man. All it ever was. It was always off the rails my guy. I saw that. Knew that. I just wish you had too."

The bar is getting brighter. Just as empty but somehow busier. Sunlight reflects off of whiskey bottles and throws amber prisms around the stage. The song continues. Coming from me as much as it is coming from him. Brandon plays on. It's hard to tell if it is closing time or if the show is about to start. Brandon looks up from his guitar and fixes me with an inquisitive stare.

"Hey? You ever end up with that Marla Singer?"

Now it's my turn to laugh. He smiles with me as he plays.

"Which one?"

"The one that matters, amigo." He says before returning back to his music. "The one that matters."

"Did you?"

He nods and motions with his chin to his guitar. The one that matters. "Maybe you should consider settling down, Saint."

"That's a bit of the pot calling the kettle coming from you Brando."

He chuckles. Two old friends in a bar. Came up together and now we're here. In this place. Wherever this place is. He gets into the guitar in

AR Bennett

earnest. Concentration playing out over his face as his fingers twist and flex against the strings.

"Hey Saint?"

"Yeah Brando?"

"Just remember man…"

The music builds and builds as the bar gets brighter and brighter. I get brighter too. Brandon Lake, missing and presumed dead lead singer of up-and-coming punk band Lake Effect in Affect, opens his mouth and

"CHAOS SCREAMS"

Track Seventeen: Dookie

A flash and a fade and then it's eyes open. Head ringing. Back to the place that is. The here and now.

Back in the Kelso Beach House.

Back home.

I come to slowly and painfully. Aware of every cut and bruise. Every painful blister and burning itchy bump. My head is pounding. Seeing stars. Tasting colors. Everything hurts everywhere all at once. Through the pain I am increasingly aware that I'm on my knees with my hands bound behind my back in tape. There's clear plastic under me that has been laid out on the floor.

I'm also aware that I'm not alone.

Goons from various allegiances move about hanging more plastic sheets from the walls. There is a Costco sized box of black trash bags on the bar. I told you properly disposing of a body is too much like hard work. And that's if you have to get rid of just one. This? This is a gathering. All the familiar faces.

There's Tommy obviously. They nabbed him when they got me. Then there's Scooby and Alaska and Young Benny Bones too. Charlie and his baseball bat grinning his Charlie Grin. His assortment of goons. Next to them is Ivan and Other Ivan with his face all smashed up with bits of bark still wedged in the bloody gaps between his teeth. The whole crew is here.

Minus Watson.

Can't blame her for wanting to be somewhere else.

Rounding the gathering out there's Colt in his suit leaning against the bar with Alisa Mikhailov and her arms wrapped around his shoulders. The blood red bottoms of her heels are an ominous bit of foreshadowing.

A proper get together.

My guys are the only ones with duct tape bracelets and kneeling on plastic sheets though.

Colt smiles the shark-like smile of a man who has gotten exactly what he wanted. Toothy grin full of malice and gloating greed.

"Turns out he's the patron saint of running out of time and out of options."

He chuckles and when his goons who are busy still hanging plastic sheets don't chuckle with him he repeats his little knee slapper until a few of the guys give halfhearted chucks and chuffs. The mafia princess of Moscow just looks annoyed. Of course she has one of those faces. Resting Bitch Face is what the kids call it I believe. These two make strange bedfellows.

Strange.

But not all that surprising.

I lift my eyes up from the plastic sheets and hold her gaze. She gets my meaning right away. With a shrug and a sly smile and the tightening of arms around ancient decrepit shoulders she responds.

"Sorry Saint. You just weren't my type anyways."

"Thanks. I was starting to piece that together on my own."

She nods. Colt nods. The goons nod. Everyone is in on the joke except for I guess maybe me. Colt gives the nonverbal command and the goons start smashing my bar. Tearing down the whiskey bottles and smashing them on the floor. I watch in silence as the mod squad dissembles my beloved speakeasy. My Kelso Beach House. My sanctuary in the storm. My place I can call my own. It's ripped apart bit by bit. Bottle by bottle.

Tommy is elbowing me in the chest, trying to tell me something important. Convey some bit of information that is inherently relevant to our current situation. It's very close and personal and in my face but it also

Feels

So

Far

Away.

Glass shatters. Brown liquors pool off the beach wood bar and onto the faded sandalwood floor. Bit by bit it all breaks. Bit by bit it all falls apart and comes undone and is shattered on the floor. My entire life, all the things I've worked so hard for comes crashing down in a toss and a throw and a chuck. All of it adding to the pile of my regrets. Once more for feeling. Once more unto the breach. It all breaks at my feet and I watch in silence as everything I have worked so hard to maintain comes apart.

Now it's Scooby's turn to elbow me in the ribs. I look at him and he jerks his square chin that-a-way back to Twelve Toes. They both seem to want to tell me something that at this moment I'm not capable of comprehending. A silent game of hot potato with me in the middle. Passing notes in class.

All around me is a chorus of my own destruction. Broken bottles. Smashed signs. Cracked bits of this and that all come crashing down at my feet. An entire symphony of my mistakes. Then there is something small and metal and rectangular being pressed into my palm. Tommy nods. Scooby nods.

They seem pleased.

Mission accomplished.

AR Bennett

They look for a sign of life behind my eyes. A clue that I am with them and present and in this moment. Something that shows that I understand the importance of what has been handed to me.

If there is a grave behind these eyes then how can the dead find a sign of life?

I don't nod. I don't do anything.

Just clutch the cold metal thing in my fingers and stare straight ahead as I see without seeing my beloved bar being ripped apart piece by piece.

Over the lake the sun starts to set. Storm clouds brew off on the horizon. It hasn't rained all scorching summer; we've spent these long days and hot nights in a perpetual state of heat induced turmoil. Losing our minds and sweating out our souls against the cracked and hot pavement. It's been a long and hard drought that we have all paid the price for.

Until now.

Somewhere in the distance over the darkening waters storm clouds build. Thunder rolls.

Enter Night.

The goons have smashed all they can smash. The tarps are taped up. The stage is set and dressed and ready for one last final act. Dim the lights. I look between Colt and Alisa and I just need to know. I have to figure it out. Make it all make sense and see the forest through the trees. Give me that at least. Give me some clarity before it all comes crashing down. I feel the words leaving my mouth before I hear them. Pulled up deep from some dark spot in my soul.

What's left and what is still available for speaking.

"What's on the tape?"

Ali answers first. Clinging on to Colts sides she has this wicked little smile that parts her red lips and a grin that spells my demise.

"What tape?"

Colt answers next. In this practiced partnered type of way. She speaks. He speaks. Choreographed and synchronized.

"If you can't find it, no one can. What's not out there in the open is left to rot at the bottom of the lake. Down in Davy Jones' locker."

I nod. Yeah, I get it. I start to see the picture on the back of the puzzle box.

"You sunk your own boat to get rid of the evidence."

It all seems so clear now. Maybe I should have seen it sooner. Colt laughs. The sharp bark of someone who has been cued up to laugh. The studio actor's laugh when the laugh track is required.

Here comes the punchline.

"Saint, I told you. I didn't do anything. My captain found himself in hot water. In the deep and over his head. Do you sympathize?"

Sure do.

Sure do.

There is nothing left in the tank. No more retorts or witty comebacks or jokes. No more smash cuts or cinema style stylizations. Just me nodding my head sadly as the curtain falls. As the scene comes to a close. As the lights dim and we all take our final bow.

He claps his hands together slowly.

The patronizing vice principal clap of a man who is handing out participation trophies.

"I gotta say though kid," Colt chuckles in his arrogant self-satisfied way. "You sure did give it your all."

"Yeah well. You can't stop a nazi with good intentions, now can you?"

"Charlie?"

"Yeah Boss?"

Hit him.

Charlie looks conflicted. He's swinging the bat between his hands in that I'm definitely unsure manner. Hesitant. I look up from the floor and basically dare Charlie to do it. Go on then. No dog like a loyal dog Charlie. Give us your worst.

"That's a bit harsh isn't it Boss?" Charlie says finally. Torn between me and his boss. Between the guy at his feet and the guy holding the girl in his arms watching the world burn around him. "He's already broken, isn't he?"

If only I had the energy to SMASH CUT to something witty. Something clever and heroic and maybe what you'd come to expect from a guy like me. But I don't. There isn't enough gas left in the tank. I just nod.

Yeah Charlie.

You're right.

He is broken.

Silencers are screwed on. Gloves are passed around and donned. The signs of violence impending have finally found a time and that time is now.

All I can think about is at least Scooby's car will be safe. He loves that car. Put all of his time and energy and paychecks for crooked jobs working crooked hours into that car. Saved up every penny he had to buy it.

The Twins will take care of it.

Keep it safe.

Be good stewards to the Golden Beast.

I think about that and think about who else I could have been a better steward to. Alaska. He deserved a better friend. Maybe one that wouldn't use his size and strength to his own advantages if the mood struck right.

And then there's Young Benny Bones.

I could have been a better example, a better role model. Lead by better doings and played the part of big brother differently. Got him out of the game. Out of harm's way. Out of this little underworld of ours. Fuck.

Above all else maybe I could have done that.

I snap my head up from the funk I'm currently drowning in. There's a bit of fire left behind these baby blues. A bit of will.

"Let them go."

Colt answers before his bonnie lass-to-be can.

"Let who go, Saint?"

I jerk my head their way. To Scooby and to Alaska and to Benny Bones. All bound in tape kneeling next to me paying the price I wagered.

"The Bad Bunch. These guys. This is all on me not on them."

Colt turns to Alisa Mikhailov, to the woman who grew up on mob hits and silenced witnesses. Whose apple hasn't fallen far from the tree. Who's a chip off the old block. A real Bad One. Born and raised and corn fed on murder the way some kids are weaned on mother's milk.

She shakes her head sadly.

"No witnesses."

Soft sub vocalizations like pillow talk. Something I'm familiar with and for the first time actually regret knowing. There's cold and then there is ice cold and this is Arctic. Shivers go down my spine.

Goosebumps fight for real estate amidst cigarette burns on my arms.

Colt nods. He's looking a bit green around the gills. A bit out of league and out of sorts. His business has never been brutality. His business has been business. Whatever the costs sure, but not this up front and personal. Not front row. Not popcorn and big sodas and technicolor. Live and in person. He nods again. Maybe to himself this time.

"I guess that's my cue." He straightens his tie around his neck and smooths out the imagined wrinkles in his suit. "I'll leave y'all too it then."

He untangles himself from Alisa's wrapped arms and slides off the bar. Motioning to Charlie to convey signals that his number one knows what to do. Charlie's not so sure but he nods anyway. This is out of bounds and out of pocket but an order is an order. Next to me Tommy really wants my attention.

He's fidgeting and spinning and spun up. Trying what he can to say what he needs to say. I slowly break eye contact with Colt as the suited man, dog number one, shuffles out from a side door of the bar.

Not even man enough to see shit through.

"Saint?" Tommy implores.

"Yeah Tommy?"

He looks sad. Sad and determined and set in whatever ideas he has formulated in his rat-like skull.

"I do think that Brandon really did try to come home. In the end."

I wanted to ask him what he means by that but he's off like a shot. One last bit of junky energy. Raging against the dying of the light. Tommy Twelve Toes, rat faced fucker and wayward manager of Lake Effect in Affect bolts upright and puts his shoulder down in a defensive line tackle stance as he charges the nearest Ivan in front of him.

It's telegraphed and predictable to the point that the Other Ivan raises his gun and takes the shot. His aim is off though. Maybe because he saw it happen in his mind's eye or because he was truly taken aback. But the shot goes wide and imbeds in the thick storm shutters sealed shut along the wall.

Tommy tackles Ivan With The Fucked Up Face and drives him with righteous rat energy to the floor where they wrestle around trading screamed insults and short jabs.

There is another

POP

POP

And Other Ivan has his brains painted Jackson Pollock Style against the clear plastic sheets hanging from the walls. First Ivan is confused. Confounded by the idea he fucked up so badly that his partner had to pay for it. Pink mists and poorly aimed shots.

Regrets

And

Remorse.

There is the stunned pause of everyone registering what just went down and then all hell breaks loose. Charlie is shouting. The goons are shouting. Guns are drawn and being waved about. Tommy has ratted off and is army crawling his way behind the bar. There's another shot, don't know from who or from where, but that kicks off a chain of events that increasingly spirals further and further off the rails.

Fish

And

AR Bennett

Barrels.

Alisa is yelling in her native tongue as Friendly Fire Ivan tries to correct himself by yanking his boss out of the fray. No longer able to tell friend from foe, Charlie is swinging his bat blindly. Gun smoke chokes the air hanging heavy with hot lead and fresh death scent.

Alaska pushes up from a crouch and throws a shoulder into a goon that stumbled too close. Knocks me back into one of his buddies who in pure slapstick fashion turns surprised and stunned and fires off a few rounds. The resident big man of the Kelso Beach House, the Bad Bunch's very own heavy, lets out a growl as a 9mm round passes over his big bicep.

Now he's pissed.

Ripping the tape off his wrists and throwing blows at anything that moves into his space.

I told you Alaska could take a round or two if need be.

Scooby is scrambling to his feet. He's yanking Benny Bones up with him and shouting for all of us to get to the door before the situation deteriorates any further. As if to punctuate that idea Tommy Twelve Toes lets out a pained scream as one of the goons puts a round low in his gut.

To me it's all just hyper HD ultra realistic cinema. Underscored and dramatized in slow motion. As Scooby yanks the Bad Bunch out the front and onto the porch I can see thick fat bolts of lightning descending down from angry dark skies over the lake. Big drops of rain leave impact craters in the sand and detonate like all the hand grenades in all the wars.

Thunder shakes the walls in rolling waves.

Above all that atmosphere the cosmic soundtrack has found the perfect song to score the ending of the world.

I watch it all unfold in front of me. Bullets ripping past my face leaving sonic trails as they cut through the slowmo air. Wood splinters flying. The slow and steady drip drip drip of whiskey leaking off the bar and soaking up into puddles on the floor. Outside I can hear my friends yelling against the storm. Their words mean nothing to me as it is just all noise.

Then there's this small metal thing in my hand.

Click

Clack

Click

Clack

Open and closed. Open and closed. My finger traces the scratches where a heart was crossed out and replaced with an "A" in a circle. The recognizable symbol for anarchy.

Tommy makes eye contact with me from where he is bleeding out on the floor. Gone is the rat. Gone is the gnaw and claw and do anything to survive. He's just a sad little guy with no more fight left to be fought. He nods his head slowly, a small smile playing out over his tight white lined lips.

Click Clack

Click Clack

Standing up takes effort. Getting from a crouch to a stand after running all night, running scared and going full tilt, is challenging. I can hear my knees creak and protest even over the sound of the screams, the storm, the soundtrack, and everything else. Chaos. Destruction. Death creeping. World still in slow motion.

I guess there's one thing left to do.

AR Bennett

Why not? We made it this far. Been a good run.

Click. Clack. Click.

Open. Closed. Open.

I flick the wheel and ignite the striker. The filter in the Zippo catches on the first spin and comes alive hot with orange fire in my hand. I drop the lit lighter down and watch it fall in agonizing slow as it lands in a puddle of brown liquor.

The vapors catch almost immediately. Then the plastic sheets. Then the walls and floors and wood. It's only a matter of seconds before everything I worked so hard to protect is burning. Up in smoke. Flames reaching higher.

Just stand in the center of it.

Watch Charlie grab a nearest or maybe dearest goon and kick out the back door.

Watch Tommy smile his little last man smiling smile and look up at the ceiling.

The bar goes up. Smashed bottles of Canadian imported booze of questionable origin pop and fizzle as their contents ignite and add to the blaze. The smoke gets thick. Hot and black and oppressive.

Watch it all burn.

The Fire and The Flames.

The Smoke and The Screams

The Patron Saint of Lost Causes.

Then there are strong scrawny arms around my chest. Yanking me backward. No more fight left to give. Low top Chuck Taylors sliding on sandalwood floors. Scooby has his shirt wrapped around his face. A makeshift mask. He's pulling me backwards out of the inferno I caused. Because of course he is.

We're partners after all.

Not that we stare into each other's eyes. Just that

One usually follows the other.

He gets me out and onto the sand just as the phantom band reaches a crescendo. Behind me the lake is coming alive with storms and waves and nature's fury. In front of me my world burns. Scoob is shouting if I'm okay? Yelling in my ear. Shaking my shoulders. I just sort of slide down him and crash into the wet sand.

The dark skies are tinted orange as the flames reach up ever higher. Somewhere down the beach I can hear sirens fighting for volume over the thunder and the storm. Rain pours down my face and washes crusted and caked on blood off my cheeks. Down my nose. Off my lips. Red and blue lights add to the oil painting of colors.

Find the one that matters.

I tried.

I fucking

…tried.

*****

It's all night before the rains stop and the storm subsides. The sun comes up over a calming lake leaving me in the same spot in the sand to stare at the smoking rubble that was once The Kelso Beach House.

Home of The Bad Bunch.

As in "Don't fall in with that crowd they're a bad bunch."

Men in thick black and yellows sift through the smoking heap. Red metal helmets dripping with the last drops of rain and hose water. Respirators on their faces against the fumes.

I feel her sit down next to me before I see her.

Watson doesn't say anything at first. Just sits in the damp sand next to me. There's a gold badge dangling from a silver chain around her neck.

Contrast to the dark black vest with big bold white letters strapped to her chest. We sit like this for an eternity. Watching the sunrise together on the beach outside the KBH just like we had done a hundred times before.

I'm the first to speak and it's barely a whisper.

"Of course you're a Donnie Brasco." Should have seen that coming. It was all just too…whatever it was.

"I'm sorry Saint." She says finally. "I said you should have left this one alone."

"This the part where you tell me it was all real?"

"We both had fun, didn't we?" She states softly. "If it makes you feel better, I wasn't here initially for you."

I nod. There isn't really much left to say. When she's right she's right. That about sums it all up.

"We got Colt. Most of his guys made it out and it looks like Charlie had a change of heart about what is the right way and bad way to conduct business. He's singing his boss out like a canary to save his own skin. Bribery. Arson. Conspiracy to commit murder. Should be more than enough."

She pauses. Watches the last glowing embers fizzle and fade out.

"The Boys are all okay. Alaska will have a nice little scar from where a bullet grazed him, and Scooby will have a bit of a cough for a minute, but otherwise they are fine. I'll keep Young Benny Bones out of all this. He's a minor after all."

Nod again. Listen without listening. There is a definiteness to the silence. A finality.

"I'm going to have to book you though." She looks at me with genuine sadness in her eyes. "Usual stuff. Operating without a license. That sort of thing. The good news is you won't do any serious time. A few fines. Maybe a week or two in The

House because of your priors. Nothing you can't handle or haven't handled before. You can say I have some serious pull with the captain."

Apples.

Trees.

Fathers and daughters.

Why not? She is connected after all.

As if reading my mind, she shakes her head slowly.

"Mikhailov got away. Went underground. But we'll find her. Your testimony will go a long way towards making sure we can put her and hers away for good. Plus, that will buy you some good will in the courts. You'll be a CI...my CI...which I know you feel a type of way about. There are rules in this little underworld of yours. But that's where we're at."

She gently stands me up and walks me to a waiting cop car. I go willingly. Walking in a zombified way that is more shuffle than actual walk. Head hung low. Compliant.

Over the next couple of days Watson tells me what to say and I say it. I'm booked. Light charges just like she said they would be. Face the camera. Turn left. Turn right. Fingers in ink and once again in the system. It's not my first stay in the slammer.

Not too bad. Quiet. I know most of the guys here anyway. We all came up together, hadn't we?

Track Eighteen: Songs to Fan the Flames of Discontent

A few weeks go by in the clink before I find myself fresh out the gate and back in Scooby's Great Golden Beast. Released onto the world. A free man once again.

He points the hood toward the beach and lets the big beefy V8 bring us home. Or what's left of it.

I'm kicking bits of charcoal and ducking under caution tape in the ruins of the Kelso Beach House, wheels turning and spinning in my head, when suddenly out of nowhere the light bulb kicks on.

Something said and half remembered. Something from that night that was gnawing and clawing at me. Keeping me up at night without really knowing why.

Home.

As in: "In the end Brandon really did try to come home."

Softly over the lake, up in the azure sky, a steady punk beat is building.

I kick my way through the debris towards the ashes of my back office. Scrape away the burnt rafters and pieces of my torched desk. Under the blackened floor, through a secret hatch, there's a fireproof safe that no one had removed because no one was looking for it.

It's right there just as it always is

And was.

I crouch down and turn the dial. Zero right. Zero left. One right. The latch releases with a clack and I pull the handle to open the heavy little metal door. The music gets louder. The camera angle switches so that you can see my bandaged and freshly healing face looking into the safe from the inside.

I pull out an envelope full of old photos. Me and Scooby in borrowed suits heading to prom with our dates. Alaska and I in our sports jerseys. Young Me and even younger Benny Bones splashing about building sandcastles while dad looks on proudly. The envelope goes into my pocket. Tucked away safe and sound.

Under that though.

There's a small box wrapped in Christmas paper. Wrapping paper in the middle of July. Makes total sense if you have the sort of junky mind. Wouldn't even think twice about it.

I make my way out of the ruins and back onto the burnt-up porch facing the lake. Ripping red and green paper as I go. Sitting under a turned over table is a slightly crispy boombox. I snag that too and sit down on the steps.

She's standing outside of the police tape. Dark hair pulled back in a bun. Golden eyes catching the sun with sparkles and shine. Hospital scrubs looking impossibly good for what they are.

"Hey." She calls taking a hesitant step forward. "Heard this place used to be the happening spot."

"It was once."

"Crazy what happened. I came from work to check it out for myself. Something out of a movie, right?"

"Are you a nurse?"

She laughs. Looks down at her scrubs as if this is the first time seeing them. Smooths out a few wrinkles. I like her laugh.

"No I uh..I work in the pharmacy."

Well, that's basically the same thing, now isn't it? Close enough. I always said if a woman can look good in scrubs, she can look good in anything. And she looks really good. Never seen her around before. Must not be in The Life.

"Do you like movies then?"

"Love them. Can't get enough."

I like movies too. Can't get enough either. Raised on them. Came up with them.

"Who are some of your favorites?"

There's that laugh again. That small smile. The way her eyes catch the sun in shades of gold. She pushes back a loose strand of hair and tucks it behind her ear.

"Oh man…tough call. There is Tarantino for sure." I nod with her. For sure. Classic. King of dialogue and modern pulp. "Guy Ritchie. Shane Black. That sort of thing."

"What do you know? Those are some of my favorites too."

Raised on them.

Came up with them.

I get up from the porch and make my way past the yellow caution tape. Duck under it and walk up to her. She sticks out her hand confidently.

"I'm Kim by the way."

I take her hand in mine and give it a little shake. Her skin is soft and smooth.

"I'm..." I look back at the ruins of the Kelso Beach House. Over my shoulder she looks past me slightly confused. Biting her lip in a way that tells me she doesn't know she does it but does when she is given reason to. Like when a guy she just met can't seem to decide his own name. Because what's in a name anyways? What's in changing one?

Starting fresh from the beginning all over again. From the ashes to new. "...I'm Andy."

"Nice to meet you, Andy."

"You too Kim. Do you like punk music?"

"Love punk music."

As do I. There is no better kind in my opinion. Speaks to the anger and rage and authoritarian pressures of youth. Builds in intensity. Volume. Decibels. Been to my fair share of punk shows. Know a few people in the scene. Couple big names. You might have heard of at least one. The fact that she likes what I like is something I didn't know that I wanted.

I put the boombox down in the sand. There's two unopened Coronas just chilling there because of course there is. I take them and blow off the sand stuck to the glass. Pop the top and hand her one. I crumple up the remaining wrapping paper and chuck it into the smoldering pile. Inside the box is a note.

"You'll fucking love it." -BL

And under the note

Is a tape.

I put the tape in the boombox's player and my finger hovers over the play button. This golden eyed girl is looking at me intrigued and curious and slightly unsure. But she hasn't left yet. She's still standing here with a warm flat beer in her hands looking at me like what's he gonna do? Who is this guy?

AR Bennett

My finger gives this little shake. Hesitation and uncertainty play out over my face.

What do I know about albums? Aren't they made in Santa Monica?

"Fuck it."

I press play and it's

SMASH CUT TO:

The Bad Bunch

By AR Bennett

Starring
Saint
Scooby
Alaska
Benny Bones
Watson

With
Barnaby Colt
Alisa Mikhailov
The Ivans & The Goons

*****

There are few places that look and feel less haunted than empty and abandoned ice cream parlors in the summer. Handsome Black sits on the hood of his Honda in the dark under a giant plaster soft serve cone fashioned to the roof of the closed Whippy Dip. He's swinging his legs and humming a tune waiting. Has been here awhile and is just about to give up and go back to the KBH when a long black SUV pulls up with Quebec plates. He hops off his car and stands in the headlights waiting for the inhabitants from the SUV to disembark.

Three men who easily could have been traveling to the States from a lumberjack conference get out and stand with Handsome in the light. "We were expecting Saint."

Handsome nods his head and smiles his million-kilowatt smile. "He's a bit tied up at the moment."

Too true Handsome. If you only knew the half of it.

"But not to worry. He's assured me that everything is fine. The next shipment will take place as scheduled."

The Lumberjack Triplets look between themselves and confer in French before turning back to Handsome Black and his smiling handsome face. "Can you guarantee that?"

"Of course I can. I'm black."

"Yes, we recognize and respect that you aboot you, eh?"

Handsome's grin drops and he turns from the Canadians to look directly at the camera.

"Damnit Saint," he says angrily. "I better get something in the sequel because this mid-credit comedy scene aint it brotha."

*****

Featuring
Nikki Sixxx
The Skittle Twins
Tommy Twelve Toes

And
Brandon Lake

Outro Track: The New Noise

FADE IN

Interior - A Butcher's Shop - Night

Big racks of bloodied meat hang from steel hooks on the wall. There are intestines and discarded orifices on the blood-stained concrete floor. A butcher in a brown leather apron uses a meat cleaver to chop slaps of raw steaks. Hacking and slashing them into smaller more manageable sections.

He is big and burly with a head of tangled hair that has traces of bone and muscle stuck in it. His chest is glistening with sweat under the apron as he works silently and methodically to chop the meat with the big, threatening, glinting cleaver. In the background a phone rings.

AR Bennett

The Butcher sets down his knife and walks to a corded phone mounted on the wall.

> THE BUTCHER
> "Da?"

Indescribable muffles speaking in Russian can be heard from the other end of the line. The Butcher listens to the conversation and nods.

> THE BUTCHER
> "Da. One minute."

He sets the phone aside and turns toward the backroom of the butcher shop. Through a door covered in thick plastic sheets a man steps out of the shadows and into the dim flickering light. THE BUTCHER holds up the phone for him before bowing his head and scurrying off into the dark past the plastic curtains.

This new man is undoubtedly Russian. Yet he doesn't look like a Bond villain. No sinister scar. No cartoonish black and white striped shirt. Just a head of hair so platinum that it reflects white in the dim light and a suit in the tens of thousands of dollars with a set of jewelry - watch, pinky rings, necklaces and chains - to match. BORIS MIKHAILOV picks up the phone and listens for a moment.

> BORIS MIKHAILOV
> "No Misha. Now this seems to be my problem. You say this man is a saint? Then I hope he prays."

A wicked smile creeps up on his face as he hangs the phone up with a definitive smack.

CUT TO BLACK

AR Bennett

Acknowledgements

Where do I even start? There are so many people who I would like to acknowledge as instrumental parts of bringing this book to life. First off, and right off the bat, I want to thank my wife. There is not a single part of this process that I could have done without you. Thank you for putting up with my insanity. Then there is my family. My brother who helped me find my pacing and tone, and my aunt, uncle, and cousins whose reassurance that my voice was there helped me keep going. Mom and Dad for telling me I could be anything.

I couldn't have gotten far without Shiloh Wenona – my editor – and Derek Hayes who had answered my S.O.S when I was in the weeds with formatting. Writers helping writers is what this is all about.

Thank you all.

Perhaps most importantly, I want to thank you – yes you – my readers. Without you Saint, Scooby, and the rest of 'The Bunch' would be nothing more than voices in my head. I hope you had just as much fun reading their stories as I had writing them. Truly. Thank you so very much.

Anyways, it's looking like it's about that time. Once more with feeling…

FADE OUT

Made in the USA
Columbia, SC
13 June 2025